WHEN THE SEA TURNED TO SILVER

WHEN THE SEA TURNED TO SILVER

Grace Lin

LITTLE, BROWN AND COMPANY
NEW YORK BOSTON

Copyright © 2016 by Grace Lin

Little, Brown and Company

Hachette Book Group
1290 Avenue of the Americas, New York, NY 10104
Visit us at lb-kids.com

Little, Brown and Company is a division of Hachette Book Group, Inc.
The Little, Brown name and logo are trademarks of Hachette Book Group, Inc.

The publisher is not responsible for websites (or their content) that are not owned by the publisher.

First Edition: October 2016

Library of Congress Cataloging-in-Publication Data

Names: Lin, Grace, author.
Title: When the sea turned to silver / Grace Lin.
Description: First edition. | New York ; Boston : Little, Brown Books for Young Readers, 2016. | Companion book to: Where the mountain meets the moon. | Summary: "Pinmei, a storyteller's granddaughter, must find the Luminous Stone that Lights the Night to rescue her grandmother, who has been kidnapped by the Tiger Emperor"—Provided by publisher. | Includes bibliographical references.
Identifiers: LCCN 2015041876 | ISBN 9780316125925 (hardback)
Subjects: | CYAC: Fairy tales. | Adventure and adventurers—Fiction. | Kidnapping—Fiction. | Grandmothers—Fiction. | Storytellers—Fiction. | China—History—Fiction. | BISAC: JUVENILE FICTION / Fairy Tales & Folklore / Adaptations. | JUVENILE FICTION / Fantasy & Magic. | JUVENILE FICTION / Historical / Asia.
Classification: LCC PZ8.L6215 Whb 2016 | DDC [Fic—dc23 LC record available at http://lccn.loc.gov/2015041876

10   9   8   7   6   5   4   3   2   1

RRD-C

Printed in the United States of America

FOR ALVINA

SPECIAL THANKS TO:
ALEX, LIBBY, ALISSA, AUSTIN, KHERYN, REBECCA,
AND THE RICHLAND LIBRARY FOR THE USE
OF THEIR FOLKTALE COLLECTION

CHAPTER

1

When the sea turned to silver and the cold chilled the light of the sun, Pinmei knew the Black Tortoise of Winter had arrived with his usual calmness. But when a shrieking wind pierced the sky, bursting it into darkness, she grew frightened. It was as if the Black Tortoise of Winter were being forced to the earth, screaming and struggling.

Even the snow, usually so gentle, flew at Pinmei's mountain hut like sharp needles before falling onto the village below. The village was filled with houses crowded together, and when villagers climbed up the mountain, their hearty laughs and stomping boots shattered the quiet. At the sound of their footsteps, Pinmei would scurry away to be out of sight, her long braid trailing her like the tail of a disappearing mouse.

The villagers used to climb up to the mountain hut regularly, requesting that Amah embroider peonies or five-colored clouds onto silks for weddings and birthdays. Even in the winter, when the rough-stone hut was all but buried, the villagers still came. However, while they came for Amah's embroidery skills, they stayed for the old woman's stories. Even Pinmei, watching from behind a door, was unable to resist her grandmother's words.

"...and when the immortal dragon picked up the beautiful white stone, it began to shine in his hands..." Amah would say, telling the Story of the Dragon's Pearl, or, "...and because only a mountain can hold up the moon, no one could lift the ball..." when telling the Story of the Boy Who Rolled the Moon, and Pinmei would find herself standing among the villagers as if pulled by a thread.

But now few villagers came up the mountain, and it was not just the winter keeping them away. The ones who did come told stories of their own. "A new emperor wears the gold silk robe," they whispered, as if afraid even up on the mountain they would be overheard. "All celebrated

when the old emperor was overthrown, but now we tremble. For the new emperor is brutal and fierce. They call him the Tiger Emperor."

"But a new emperor is supposed to pay tribute to the mountain!" Amah said. "He must get the blessing of the Mountain Spirit at the top! We have not seen anyone."

"Do we ever see any rulers?" Yishan said in a scoffing tone only a young boy such as himself could have. Even though he had his own hut farther up the mountain, Yishan claimed the seat by the fireplace in Pinmei's hut as his own. "They all say they go to the top, but do they?"

"He came," one villager said, "and he started up the mountain. But the wind or the winter—or who knows, maybe even the Mountain Spirit—forced him down, to our great misfortune. He was humiliated, and now all the mountain villages are being punished."

"But reaching the top of the mountain has nothing to do with the villages!" Amah said. "It is the Spirit of the Mountain who decides if the ruler is worthy!"

"That does not matter to the Tiger Emperor," the villager said, the bitterness cracking the hushed tone of his voice. "His soldiers come to the villages late at night, taking away all the men. We do not know when they will come to ours, but we know they will."

"All the men?" Amah gasped. "What for?"

"For the Vast Wall," another villager said. "The men are being forced to build a wall that surrounds the entire kingdom."

The entire kingdom was hundreds of cities and thousands of villages! Amah often told stories about a city with a wall around it, and Pinmei could scarcely imagine that.

"You can't build a wall that long! It's impossible!" Yishan said. The firelight made his hat glow as if he were aflame.

The villager shrugged. "This emperor has a habit of making the impossible happen."

"But even if it could be finished, it would be poor protection," Amah said. "How could a wall spanning the kingdom be defended? There would never be enough soldiers to guard something so vast! What does this Tiger Emperor want?"

"He wants a Luminous Stone," said a third villager, speaking for the first time. "When anyone—a wife, a child, a mother—begs for a man's freedom, the soldiers always say the same. 'Bring the emperor a Luminous Stone That Lights the Night and you can have your wish.'"

"A Luminous Stone That Lights the Night," Amah repeated slowly. She hesitated, and Pinmei thought she saw a flash over Amah's face. But Amah shook her head. "I've never heard of such a thing."

Disappointment flickered on the faces of the villagers. The first villager reached out his hand to Amah for his completed job, a cloth embroidered with the dark blue color of a burial robe.

"No one has," the villager said. "But now we all wish for one."

The villagers left in silence, but their words remained loud in Pinmei's ears. *Luminous Stone, Vast Wall, Tiger Emperor*... Another gust of icy air burst through the open door. Shivering, Pinmei crept deeper into the shadows of the fire, hoping to hide.

CHAPTER
2

Pinmei had not realized how long it had been winter until she was getting the rice for dinner. When she reached into the jar, her fingers touched the bottom of the container.

Pinmei drew back her hand as if stung. It was too soon! She was only supposed to feel that smooth base when the tree tips were green and the swallows were awake and singing. But the breath of the Black Tortoise of Winter was still shaking the bare tree branches, and the birds were still as asleep as mussels deep in the sea.

"Pinmei!" Amah called. "What are you doing? Where's the rice?"

Pinmei grabbed a bowl and filled it. As she brought it to Amah, her grandmother shook her head.

"We shouldn't be using that bowl, Pinmei," Amah said, and Pinmei realized she was holding the blue rice bowl with the white rabbit painted on it.

"Sorry," Pinmei said.

"You know that bowl is only for special occasions," Amah said. "My grandfather—"

"Received it from the king of the City of Bright Moonlight," Pinmei finished, an impish smile curving. "But he wasn't the king yet when your grandfather got it, so I don't think it counts as a royal gift."

"You only tease your poor grandmother when we are alone." Amah pretended to sigh. "When I tell people how you taunt an old woman, they don't believe me. 'Little Pinmei?' they say. 'She's just a shy little mouse.'"

Pinmei made a face as Amah grinned at her. It was true that now, alone with Amah, her words did not freeze in her throat. She didn't know why, at the sight of anyone unfamiliar, she felt like a fish trapped in a bowl of ice, unable to even gasp for air.

"An old grandmother is not enough company for a child," Amah said, her smile fading. "Maybe trying to keep you safe by living up on this high mountain is selfish."

"Yishan lives even higher," Pinmei said. "You can even see the sea from where he lives. And above him, at the very top, is the Mountain Spirit. But we never see him."

Pinmei looked at her grandmother. "Why don't we ever see the Mountain Spirit?" Pinmei asked. "You'd think we would because we live on the mountain."

"We do see him," Amah said. "You know, the Mountain Spirit is also called the Old Man of the Moon. So you see him every time you look at the moon."

"That's not what I meant," Pinmei said. "I meant seeing him the way emperors are supposed to when they pay tribute to the mountain—as an old man talking to them."

"And what would you say to him?" Amah teased. "My quiet girl who just squeaks and hides?"

Pinmei flushed. She often wished she were like Yishan, who spoke as if each of his words were carved in stone. Or like Amah, who seemed to weave silk threads with her voice.

"Do you wish I were different?" Pinmei asked.

"Different?" Amah asked. "How?"

Pinmei shrugged, embarrassed. "Maybe if I talked more or did things," Pinmei said. "Like Yishan."

"I never wish for you to be anyone except yourself," Amah said, looking into Pinmei's eyes. "I know that when it is time for you to do something, you will do it."

Pinmei looked at the rice Amah had washed, a drop of water rolling down the side of the bowl like a single tear.

"Besides," Amah said, "you shouldn't compare yourself to Yishan. He…"

"'He' what?" Pinmei asked, raising her head.

"Oh, he doesn't remember everything he knows—that's all," Amah said. "He forgets a lot. Like now, he forgets he's only a young boy."

"Why doesn't Yishan just live with us?" Pinmei asked. "He comes here all the time."

"He doesn't want to," Amah asked. "I asked him right after Auntie Meiya died."

The wind began to wail, filling the hut with a mournful sound. Pinmei felt the stinging feeling of the rice jar return, its numbness spreading over her. It had been right after Auntie Meiya's death that winter had come. And ever since, Yishan had lived alone in his hut.

"Amah," Pinmei said slowly, "it has been winter for a long time."

"Yes." Amah nodded. "I've never known the Black Tortoise of Winter to stay so long before."

"The Black Tortoise will leave though, right?" Pinmei asked. "It can't stay winter forever."

"He will leave," Amah said confidently. "The Black Tortoise will wish to go home eventually."

Will he leave before the rice jar is completely empty? Pinmei thought. The wind was howling now, and Pinmei could see the tree branches clawing at the darkening sky. She swallowed and said, "Couldn't someone get the Black Tortoise to go home now?"

"The Black Tortoise is very strong and very mighty," Amah said. "It is his little brother's feet that hold up the sky."

"Hold up the sky?" Pinmei asked.

"What? You know this story!" Amah smiled, and, for the moment, winter was forgotten.

THE STORY OF NUWA

Long ago, the four pillars of the sky collapsed. Without their support, the sky burst apart, and the Starry River crashed down, flooding the entire earth. Countless people and animals perished in the deluge, and sea demons emerged and began devouring those still alive. All cried for mercy. But with the heavens also in turmoil, all the immortals were too concerned with their own affairs to attend to the ones on earth.

All the immortals, that is, except one. Nuwa, the goddess who instead of legs had a tail like a fish, heard the cries from earth. She looked below and gasped in horror.

When she saw a monstrous turtle destroy a hundred villages with each step of his foot, she flew down in a fury and slew it with her sword. Then, just as quickly, she sliced its legs off and used each limb to replace the broken pillars. The legs turned to stone and became the four great mountains of the land.

However, even though the sky was now supported, it was still broken. The Starry River gushed through the holes, flooding the earth. Nuwa gathered stones of five colors and shoved them into each opening. But she could not find a stone to fill the largest gap. The water dislodged every rock she tried to place in the gash, each failure creating more death.

Nuwa saw the devastation and knew what she must do. She looked at her husband, Fuxi, in the distance, and a single tear fell from her eye.

"Goodbye," Nuwa whispered.

At that moment, Fuxi realized what was happening. "Nuwa!" he shouted, his hands grabbing.

It was too late. Nuwa slipped from his grasp and thrust herself into the hole in the sky. In an instant, her body turned to stone.

Fuxi stared. Clasped in his fingers was only a single strand of Nuwa's hair, a tiny drop of blood falling from it. His wife was gone.

Fuxi bellowed a sound of grief, a thunder that shook the heavens and four new mountains of the earth. But the Starry River flooded no more.

"The turtle that Nuwa slew," Amah finished, "was the younger brother of the Black Tortoise of Winter. His little brother's feet turned into mountains strong enough to hold up the sky. Imagine how powerful the Black Tortoise must be! So when you ask if anyone could make him go home ... well, if one could make the Black Tortoise do anything, that person would be invincible."

"Why don't we ever see the Black Tortoise, then?" Pinmei said. "If he's so big, he would be hard to miss."

"The Black Tortoise brings winter, just as the dragon

brings spring," Amah said. "Only the most honored animals are chosen for the job."

"And that makes them invisible?" asked Pinmei.

"Yes," Amah said in a tone so unusual Pinmei looked up.

"Amah," Pinmei said, "how do you know this?"

"Oh," Amah said, "a friend told me."

She lifted the cover from the pot of rice, and steam rose like a thick smoke, veiling her face.

"Amah, these stories aren't real, are they?" Pinmei asked. "Was there really a tortoise or a Nuwa?"

Amah spooned the rice from the pot. She handed Pinmei her plain bowl, the cooked grains shining like a mound of pearls against the dark pottery.

"They say when you see a rainbow in the sky, you are seeing Nuwa and the colored stones she put there," Amah said. She gave Pinmei a smile, her face wrinkling like the pit of a peach. "Whether you believe that or any of the things I tell you is up to you."

CHAPTER

3

"Wake up, Pinmei! Wake up!"

Pinmei's eyes opened more from the urgency in Amah's voice than the shaking of her shoulders. In the blackness of the room, Amah's face was a thin sliver above her, like the moon on its last night. "Come quickly!"

"Amah?" Pinmei said. "What..."

"Shhh!" Amah said. The softness of her voice was unable to hide its intensity, and she was already pushing Pinmei into the darkness. "Not a word! Hurry!"

Pinmei looked at Amah's face for answers but could see only its bare outline in the shadows. In the unlit rooms, the night was as solid as lacquered wood. Pinmei wondered why Amah did not light a lantern. She silently stumbled as Amah dragged her to the hut's storage room, the freezing drafts biting her feet.

But those bare feet that knew the feel of the mountain also felt something else. There was a slight rhythmic trembling—as if the ground itself were scared. Suddenly, Pinmei knew why Amah had not brought out a lantern. Someone was coming.

"In here!" Amah said, pushing Pinmei toward a huge vat.

"In the old *gang*?" Pinmei said. The giant clay container had once held wine, but now it was empty and cracking. It sat in the storage room only because it was too big for Amah to get rid of.

"It now has a use," Amah said as she hoisted Pinmei up. "As does your quietness. Now is the time to use your gift of silence, Pinmei."

"Amah," Pinmei protested, "what—"

"The mountain is not stopping them from coming," Amah said, more to herself than to Pinmei. "Perhaps there are too many or it does not dare, for it might injure those who are blameless. But Yishan will watch out for you."

"Yishan?" Pinmei asked. "Why—"

"Remember," Amah said, shushing her, "you can always

trust Yishan." Ignoring the rest of Pinmei's protests, she gently but firmly pushed Pinmei down inside the *gang*.

Pinmei clutched her knees, grimacing as the grime of decades rubbed against her. She twisted in the vat, the rough pottery scratching her cheek, but she was rewarded by a good-sized crack at eye level. She saw Amah swiftly shuffling baskets and boxes to further hide the *gang*.

"Amah," Pinmei whispered, "where will you hide?"

Instead of answering, Amah came to the *gang* and rested her hand on Pinmei's head. Through the crack, Pinmei saw the worn knot of Amah's sash. The frayed threads, like delicate hairs of a newborn child, caught the dim light from the doorway.

"My quiet girl," Amah said softly. And then, silently, Amah took a large platter, placed it over the *gang*'s opening, and left.

CHAPTER

4

They came like thunder.

The wind and sky were eerily quiet, so, even with the muffling snow, the thumping echoed. The baskets and pots Amah had placed on the floor near the *gang* trembled as the beating came closer. When they finally arrived, they seemed to crash into the house, for the front door clattered to the floor like a fallen tree. Even though Pinmei couldn't see much from the *gang*, she squeezed her eyes shut.

Then there were men's voices, rough, harsh, commanding. When Pinmei finally dared to open her eyes, the crack in the *gang* let her see the angry fires of the soldiers' torches. The orange flames made the men and horses glow like demons.

Then Pinmei gasped, for there was Amah. She stood in the open doorway, as if waiting.

"Good evening," Amah said, her low voice spilling into the crowd, like a stream of water. "I hope you did not abuse your horses just to reach this old body."

"That's her!" a rough voice roared through the cold night. "She's the one we want! Take her!"

His soldiers come to the villages late at night, taking away all the men, the villagers had said. Were the soldiers here for Amah? Why? She wasn't a young man!

"Shall we go, then?" Amah said, as if asking Pinmei to gather firewood. Amah's silhouette was still and calm against the flickering light of the flames. The ocean of shadows swayed in a mad dance around her.

In response, the soldiers growled in unison, the sound swelling into a snarl.

And then, in a swift, brutal motion, like a monstrous snake swallowing its prey, the men swept Amah into the blackness of the night.

CHAPTER
5

Pinmei could do nothing. As she stared, her arms, her legs, her body froze into the cold stone of the *gang*. She could not even whisper the desperate, wailing cry that throbbed in her chest.

Soldiers began to bang into the hut. They lit the lanterns, and Pinmei could see everything as if it were a stage. Once, when she was younger, Amah had taken her down to the village to see some traveling entertainers, and Pinmei felt as if she were watching a performance again. But this show was a nightmare. The soldiers overturned the tables and chairs, and Amah's carefully organized box of threads and sewing tools were strewn on the floor, red silk lying on the ground like a pool of blood.

"There's not enough room in this hovel for more than two of us!" said one man, his elaborate armor and demeanor marking him as the commander. "You, stay," he barked, motioning to a soldier in green. "Everyone else, out!"

When all the others had left, the commander turned to the remaining soldier with a transformed manner.

"Your Exalted Majesty," the commander said, bowing his head. "We have the Storyteller. Was there another purpose for your honorable presence on this excursion?"

The soldier took off his helmet, and Pinmei could see he was much older than the commander. His pointed beard was veined with white, as were his eyebrows, arched like poisonous centipedes. She also saw that his uniform was slightly ill fitting, his girth stretching the scales of his armor. He must be a king or some other royalty in disguise.

"The old woman gave up too easily," he said, his voice low and harsh. "She's trying to hide something."

He scanned the walls and shelves and floors, stepping

deliberately. As he kicked aside a small bamboo container, needles spilled out. Their sharp points glittered in the lamplight, and the king (or whoever he was) pulled at the scarf around his neck and clutched at his collar. He crossed into the storage room, the other man following.

Their steps came closer and closer to Pinmei, each thud of their boots echoing the pounding of her heart. The smell of cold and horse and oiled leather filled her nose, and she could see the lacings of each small plate of their armor.

"What is that?" The king breathed sharply and stopped directly in front of the *gang*. Pinmei's breath left her, yet she couldn't look away or even close her eyes. The king bent over, and if he had been looking at the *gang*, he could have seen Pinmei through the crack, her eyes fixed upon him like those of a trapped mouse.

But the king was not looking at the *gang*; he was looking over it. And he was staring with such intensity the air around him seemed to crackle. With a sudden forceful movement, he reached out his arm, his collar falling open so Pinmei could see a silver pin sticking out from the imperial gold silk of his hidden robe. *Imperial gold silk?*

That meant this pretend soldier was not just a king—he was the king of all the kings! He was the emperor!

"This is mine!" the emperor said with an anger that would have surprised Pinmei had she been capable of feeling any more shock. He was holding the blue rice bowl with the white rabbit painted on it.

CHAPTER

6

"Yes, Your Exalted Majesty," the commander said as the emperor handed the bowl to him. He held it as if it were made of eggshells, and Pinmei could see it took great effort for the commander not to prostrate himself on the floor. "Was there anything else?"

The emperor looked around the hut as if it smelled of rotten fish. "No," he said in disgust. "Take the old woman, and join the other troops at the bottom of this accursed mountain."

At that moment, a loud clamor sounded outside the hut. The emperor replaced his helmet as the commander strode to the doorway.

"What's the problem?" the commander snapped.

There was a brief sound of a struggle, and a soldier entered. "Just this boy," he said, shoving a small figure forward so he fell into the room. *Yishan!*

It looked as if the entire cavalry had trampled on him, for his filthy shirt was the color of soot. His hat was gone— but his head, also grime spattered, was raised high. The commander waved the soldier away with his hand.

"Do not take her!" Yishan said angrily, as if continuing a conversation.

The emperor and the commander laughed. "Here is a small pup pretending to be a dog," the emperor mocked.

Yishan's face flushed, but he still did not bow his head. "At least it's more honorable than a tiger pretending to be a man," he said, his eyes flashing.

The laughter stopped. Even under the soldier's helmet, Pinmei could see the emperor's eyes narrow. In two ferocious strides, the emperor seized and lifted the boy as if he were an animal the emperor planned to slaughter. The emperor's eyes scanned Yishan intently, from his muck-covered robes to his grubby face and matted hair. A faint, foul smell of horse dung drifted from the boy. The emperor snorted in disgust.

"You're just another dirty turtle egg, like all the

others," he growled. "You want the old woman? Bring the emperor a Luminous Stone That Lights the Night, and you can have her."

And, as if Yishan were no more than a sack of rice, he tossed the boy to the floor. He retucked his scarf around his neck, and he spat out his next words like venom.

"Burn the place," he said.

CHAPTER
7

Pinmei felt like the walls of the *gang* were pressing into her, forcing the air from her lungs. *Burn the place? Burn the hut?* Her home? As the men left the hut and the night filled with noises of bellowed orders, horses, and stomping boots, Pinmei squeezed her head into her knees, the blackness creeping over her as she trembled.

"Pinmei! Pinmei!" Yishan was whispering desperately. "Where are you?"

Her throat refused to make a noise, but Pinmei's quaking hand reached upward. The tray Amah had placed over the *gang*'s opening clattered to the floor, and in seconds Yishan was dragging Pinmei out of the *gang*.

"Pinmei!" Yishan said, shaking her. "We have to get out of here! Do you hear me?"

Pinmei nodded. The icy thatched roof made a sizzling sound, and she realized it was already beginning to flame. "They're burning the hut," Pinmei whispered.

"This hut is made of mountain stone," Yishan told her. "It won't burn fast, but we still have to leave."

Pinmei looked at the door and windows and could see only the lit torches, balls of fire rolling and spinning madly around the house like toy yo-yos.

"How?" she asked helplessly.

Yishan, standing on a storage box, was already sweeping the bowls and cups off the shelves above the *gang*, letting them smash to pieces on the floor. Fiercely, he ripped the shelves off the wall, revealing a window closed in with ancient shutters and dirt. He grabbed a plank to cover the opening of the *gang*, pulled himself up to sit on it, and began to kick at the window with such force the dirt flew over Pinmei like rain.

Torches flew into the front room, crashing against the walls. As one rolled into the pile of fallen silk, Pinmei stared as the fabric smoldered and curled, the flames sputtering as if gasping.

Just as the burning smell began to choke her, a cold, clean wind blew. Yishan had succeeded. A square of night sky, the same deep blue of the stolen rabbit rice bowl, was framed on the storage room wall.

"Come!" Yishan said, thrusting his hand at her almost violently.

Pinmei took another look at her home, but only a sea of flames, crackling orange and red, met her eyes.

"Pinmei!" Yishan said again.

She turned toward him, and he grabbed her hands.

CHAPTER
8

In the morning, the angry wind returned with the sun. Even inside the thick walls of Yishan's hut, Pinmei could hear its constant roaring, like the crashing waves of a sea storm. She sat silently, listening to it.

"You should eat something," Yishan said, handing her a small bowl of rice.

Pinmei remembered the clutching hands around Amah's prized bowl. *This is mine*, he had said.

"He was the emperor," Pinmei said, closing her eyes as the violence of the evening washed over her.

"Who was the emperor?" Yishan said.

Pinmei opened her eyes. The white steam from her rice gently reached toward her, its heat warming her hands.

"That soldier in green," she said.

"The one who threw me as if I were an empty gourd?" Yishan asked. "What about him?"

Stuttering, Pinmei told Yishan what she had seen.

"But why did he take Amah?" Yishan said after Pinmei had finished. "He wouldn't take her to work on the wall. What does he want?"

"He wants a Luminous Stone That Lights the Night," Pinmei said slowly, remembering the glint in Amah's eyes. "Maybe he thinks she can get it for him."

"Yes, a Luminous Stone..." Yishan said, his voice trailing. His clothes, still slightly damp from their recent washing, had returned to their usual cinnabar color. "I wish I could remember."

"Remember what?" Pinmei asked.

"If only I could remember..." Yishan started and stopped to look at Pinmei. "I feel like I should know what a Luminous Stone is. There must be a way we could find out."

Pinmei shrugged. "It's not as if we have the Paper of Answers, like in Amah's story," she said.

"I don't remember that either," Yishan said. "What's the Paper of Answers?"

THE STORY OF THE PAPER OF ANSWERS

L ong ago, when the City of Bright Moonlight was called the City of Far Remote, the new king arrived. He was about to marry one of the emperor's granddaughters, and with the marriage he would be given rule of the city.

It did not seem much of a gift. The bordering Jade River constantly flooded, sweeping away the strongest of walls as if flicking a lock of hair. Those who survived the floods lived in poverty and despair.

When the new king first surveyed the land that was soon to be his, he must have felt resentment to be ruler of such a place. However, when his men accidentally knocked over an old bent man carrying buckets of water, the king insisted on stopping. To everyone's great surprise, the king gave the man his arm and picked up the fallen buckets.

"Let me help you with these," the new king said. "Do you fill these at that well over there?"

"You are very kind," the old man said. Even though most nobles were not known for their strength, the king lifted the heavy buckets of water with ease. "Carrying water is not easy work."

"I've done this before," the king told him, "and you remind me of an old friend."

"Do I, now?" the old man said to him. The king bowed goodbye and returned to his sedan chair. Just as the chair began to move away, the old man caught the king's sleeve.

"If I were an old friend of yours," the old man whispered, "I would tell you that when your father offers you a wedding gift, say you want the paper inside the mouth of his tiger statue."

The new king stared openmouthed, but the sedan chair was already moving at a gallop. And when the king turned back to look, the old man was gone.

So that evening, when his father offered a wedding gift, the young king asked for the paper inside the mouth of the tiger statue. His father was taken aback, for not only had he forgotten about the paper, but he also considered it completely worthless. But the new king insisted he wanted only the paper and nothing else, so it became his gift.

At first, the king's father seemed to be right about the paper. As the king sat at his desk by the window, trying to smooth its many creases (his father had crumpled it into a ball before shoving it into the mouth of the stone tiger), he did not see anything unusual about it.

The king sighed and pushed away the paper. He had larger troubles to think about. The prior king had left many problems. His walls had been the strongest walls ever built, but they, too, had been easily destroyed by the Jade River. And the old king, afraid the desperation would lead the people into disorder, had imposed strict laws with harsh punishments. As a result, the full prisons were threatening to overwhelm the guards, and there were also whispers of revolt. Was all lost before he had even begun? The new king placed his head in his hands to think, and when the sun fell, he still had not moved.

It was in the light of the moon that the king finally stirred. As he lifted his head, he glanced at the paper. Then he stared. The paper had changed.

On the paper was a line of words in a language the king did not know. As he puzzled over the words, a cloud covered the moon and they disappeared from the page. Just as the king began to curse himself, the cloud drifted and the words reappeared. *The words only appear in the bright moonlight*, the king realized.

After much effort, the king finally deciphered the words: *You are a leader only to those who choose to follow.*

What did that mean? Days passed but the king refused to believe it was nonsense. So when he watched his men begin to build another wall to try to hold back the Jade River, the solution came to him. The old king had tried to control the water and the people with force, a method that was eventually doomed to fail. The new king realized he could not fight the water. He had to lead the water to where he wished it to go and let the water follow.

Immediately, the new king ordered the men to stop building the wall. Instead, he began plans for ditches and outlets for the river. The water became irrigation for farmland around the city.

The floods subsided. The king made a series of proclamations encouraging building, trade, and virtue. Prosperity and peace came to the city, and slowly it became one of the most magnificent cities of the land, perhaps even outshining the emperor's Capital City. The king often consulted the paper and quickly became famous for his wisdom. He renamed the city the City of Bright Moonlight, in honor of the light that revealed the words of the Paper of Answers.

"So the great City of Bright Moonlight was built because of a paper," Yishan said after Pinmei ended the story.

"Well, it was a magic paper," Pinmei said, but most of the despair had left her. Perhaps telling Amah's story was magic as well, for Pinmei felt strengthened.

"And is the Paper still there?" Yishan asked.

"No, Amah said the Paper was given away and…" Pinmei sat up. "Yishan," Pinmei continued slowly, "there's no Paper in the City of Bright Moonlight, but there is a dragon's pearl. Amah told me one of the kings of Bright Moonlight gave away the Paper of Answers and received a dragon's pearl in return!"

Pinmei's rice spilled onto her lap, but neither she nor Yishan noticed.

"A dragon's pearl?" Yishan said. "Dragon's pearls glow! A dragon's pearl—"

"Could be a Luminous Stone That Lights the Night!" Pinmei finished.

"Then let's go to the City of Bright Moonlight," Yishan said, "and get that dragon's pearl!"

"But it might not be!" Pinmei protested. "I just said a dragon's pearl *could* be a Luminous Stone!"

"Well, we should go to the city and see," Yishan said. "It's our best chance of saving Amah!"

"But—but—" stuttered Pinmei. A hundred thoughts flew into her mind like a flock of upset crows. *Go to the city? Save Amah? We couldn't. I couldn't.*

"Pinmei!" Yishan said in frustration. "You think and think and watch and watch. When are you going to stop watching? It's time to do something!"

When it is time for you to do something, you will do it, Amah had said. Pinmei closed her eyes, imagining Amah's face gazing at her, as steady and gentle as the moon. When Pinmei looked up, Yishan's eyes were piercing hers, daring and encouraging at the same time.

"All right," Pinmei said. "Let's go."

CHAPTER

9

"Do you even know how to get to the City of Bright Moonlight?" Pinmei asked. The snow fell upon them softly, like sifted salt, and their footsteps quietly thumped as they walked.

"Of course," Yishan said. "You don't?"

Pinmei shook her head. "I don't remember," she said. She could count the number of times she had been down the mountain on her hand. "Whose boots are these? They seem a hundred years old!"

Before they had left his hut, Yishan had tossed some robes and boots at her from a chest that looked as ancient as the *gang* Pinmei had hidden in. It had been almost comical how fast Yishan had moved once Pinmei had agreed to go. He had jumped up as if he were a lit fire-cracker, running into the other room, collecting food and clothes. *I guess he's afraid I'll change my mind*, Pinmei had thought with a wry smile.

"They're Meiya's, from when she was a girl," Yishan said, his voice muffled as he pushed ahead of her to lead.

Auntie Meiya. Pinmei felt as if the water she had sipped was freezing in her stomach. *Amah is alive*, Pinmei told herself fiercely. Yishan could not say the same about Auntie Meiya. Before Pinmei could say anything aloud, Yishan called out, "There's your hut! Maybe you can get some of your own stuff there."

As they got closer, they both saw how unlikely that was. The stones of the hut walls were charred, while the remains of the burned chairs and tables lay strewn on the floor. A dark, brittle ash flew in the air like dying moths.

Pinmei stood and cried. Was that scorched mass in the corner her bed? And was that crumbling mound of cinders all that was left of her clothes? Her tears flowed and flowed as if they were still trying to extinguish the already-departed flames, and the freezing wind wrapped around her. Yishan stood behind, awkwardly patting her arm.

"It's not that bad," he said unconvincingly. "I'll look around."

Pinmei said nothing and found herself staring at the old *gang*, blackened where flames had licked it. Had it only been last night? She could still feel Amah's gentle hand on her head, the soft weight of it anchoring her. Pinmei tried to wipe away her tears.

"I found something," Yishan said, his voice startling her. "Look!"

Pinmei ran to him, standing in what used to be Amah's room. He was bending over a box, burned almost beyond recognition. The cover fell to pieces as he held it up, but inside was something Pinmei had never seen before. It was a quilted jacket made of hundreds of different-colored patches. The colors were so vivid in the bleakness of the ruins that the jacket seemed to glow. As Pinmei reached to take it, something fell from its sleeve. Both Pinmei and Yishan stared at the green circle in the snow. It was a jade bracelet.

CHAPTER
10

His eyes were closed. Every time he opened them, there was a brightness so dazzling his eyes felt as if needles were pricking them.

What had happened? He had been floating lazily in the Lake of Heavens. The black water was lapping against his giant shell, and the twinkling fishes were swimming around him.

Then, from nowhere, he was thrust into the water. Down he plunged, deeper and deeper. He had screeched and thrashed, but no matter how he struggled, he was forced downward. The water thinned. His arms and legs lashed out, but his claws were as useless as knots of thread. The glaring color poured around him.

What was this place?

He forced his eyes to stay open, making them adjust to the brightness.

Gold.

All he saw was the color gold. A garish, dazzling gold that gleamed and flashed.

He winced and tried to move away, but his arms and legs shoved only silken air. It was then that he felt the heaviness on his back. Something was holding him down!

Was he a prisoner?

CHAPTER
11

Amah's limbs ached with weariness. Bound and flanked by the iron arms of a soldier, she wasn't used to the jerking motion of a galloping horse, and now that they had stopped, she felt her arms and legs tremble. Yet, despite their curtness, the soldiers, surprisingly, had not been rough with her. They were kinder to her than they were to the long line of chained men staggering together. Those prisoners had been yelled at and whipped mercilessly, and Amah would have wept if she were not so horrified.

A soldier lifted her off the horse. "Come, Storyteller," he said. "We are stopping for the night."

Soon she found herself alone in a tent. A luxury, she realized, when compared with the soldiers crowded in their shared tents or the prisoners left to huddle together without shelter. She shivered for them, listening to their moans and cries. Quietly, another soldier entered with a small torch, unbound her hands, and offered her a cake.

"Eat," the soldier said.

Amah looked and saw it was a half-eaten portion of a soldier's ration. It was his own food he was sharing. "You are kind to remember me," she said as she took it.

"You are the Storyteller," he replied as if answering a question. After she had finished eating, he tied her hands again almost with reluctance.

Another soldier burst into the tent. He was in green, and was older and larger than any of the other soldiers.

"What are you doing here?" he asked the first soldier, a menacing, low roar beginning to sound in his throat.

"He was the only one who answered me," Amah said, trying her best to sound like a petulant child. "Do you plan to starve an old woman?"

The soldier in green looked at Amah, and a shock ran through her. Eyes full of anger and power, almost to madness... Where had she seen eyes like that before?

"I will take care of her," he said to the other soldier. "Leave."

When the soldier left, the man in green took off his helmet. He looked at Amah closely, his eyes boring into her face as if searching. She looked back at him, the rigid tilt of his head telling her it rarely bowed.

"You are not just a soldier," Amah said to him. The roar of his voice echoed in her ears, calling up a strange fear she had not felt since she was a child.

"And you are not just an old woman," he spat back. "Everyone knows you! Every corner of this land has heard a tale you have whispered. Even now, the men outside wish they could sit like small children at your feet!"

The tent flapped open, and the low melancholy moan of the wind blew tiny snowflakes, like silver seeds, over Amah.

"What do you wish from me?" Amah said. She spoke slowly and carefully, swallowing to hide her dread.

"What does one always want from the Storyteller?" The man laughed with harshness. "A story, of course. Tell me the Story of the Ginseng Boy."

The Story of the Ginseng Boy? Amah swallowed her gasp of surprise. She would never forget when she had told it last. Auntie Meiya had requested that story; now it seemed so long ago. Amah closed her eyes, remembering.

"Tell me the Story of the Ginseng Boy," Auntie Meiya said. She was lying in bed, smiling, and her many wrinkles

could not hide the light in her eyes. But the hand she laid in Amah's was weak and almost transparent.

"It's the last story I wish to hear before I die," Auntie Meiya said. She looked at Pinmei and Yishan, also standing by her bed. "When you are as old as me, you are just happy you have friends to say goodbye to."

"But..." Yishan protested. "But..."

"Yishan," Auntie Meiya said, her smile melting away as she looked at him. "It is time. You are young and you will grow older every day. I will see my parents and old friends who have been gone from my life for so long. I will miss you, but it is time to end our string."

Yishan bowed his head.

"Please," Meiya said to Amah. "Tell me the story."

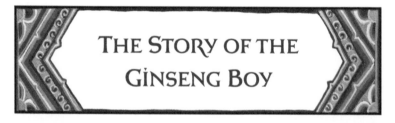

THE STORY OF THE GINSENG BOY

A long time ago, a little girl was sent away to live with an old aunt and uncle at the foot of a mountain. She had loved her small village. There had been green fields, a lake with a happy, joyful fish, and friends and parents. Here, there was only gray rock, a shadowy forest, and two old people. While the old people were not unkind, they were not interested in the girl—they spent most of their time telling her to hush or to leave them alone.

However, even the most lax of guardians could not help but notice when the girl began to eagerly leave the house. Every once in a while, when the old people looked up from their checkers game, they thought they could hear faint peals of laughter. So one morning, as the girl was rushing out the door, the aunt stopped her.

"Where are you going?" the old woman asked.

"I'm going to play!" the girl said, eager to leave.

"There's no one around here for miles," the aunt said. "A little girl like you can't play by herself all day."

"I don't," the girl said. "I have a friend!"

"A friend?" the uncle asked. "What friend?"

"A boy," the girl said. "He wears a red hat."

"A red hat?" the aunt said, and in her wonder she loosened her hold on the girl, who quickly slipped away. As the girl's figure disappeared, the two old people looked at each other.

"Did you hear that, old man?" the woman said, drops of spit sputtering from her mouth with her words. "A boy, a red hat? Here?"

"Could it be the Ginseng Boy?" the man replied, licking his lips as if hungry.

"Be patient," the woman scolded. "We have to wait for the night of the red moon."

The old people said nothing, allowing the little girl to do as she pleased. They watched the moon carefully and calculated calendar days with more fervor than when they added up their gambling tabs. Finally, one day, they cautiously followed the little girl as she left. From a distance, they watched as she rounded the house. Then a little boy appeared. He was dressed in bright red from head to foot.

"It is the Ginseng Boy!" the man said.

"Shhh!" the woman said angrily. "Keep quiet!"

The two children played for quite a while, climbing trees and drawing in the dirt. Finally, at noon, they sat against a tree and fell asleep together.

"Now!" the woman hissed.

The two old people crept forward silently. With a small knife, the old woman cut a sleeve of the boy's shirt and pulled a delicate red thread. The old man tied it tightly to a low branch of a bush. They nodded to each other and, just as silently as before, departed.

That night, the moon shone blood red and the old man and his wife left the house, each with a lantern and a spade. With much stumbling, they found the string tied to the branch and began to follow it—around trees, over rocks, through bushes, until, at last, at the foot of the mountain, the thread went right into the ground. With great haste, the old people began to dig.

"Here!" the man said, stopping his frenzied digging. He held his lantern and stared. In the hole was a large root shaped like a child. The thread led to a piece of cloth wrapped around one of the arms of the root—the remaining part of the boy's unraveled shirt.

"It is the Ginseng Boy!" the woman hissed.

They dropped their spades in a clatter, grabbed the root, and hurried home. They rushed into the house with such glee it woke up the small girl. Having never heard such delighted noises from her relatives before, the girl got out of bed and was astonished to see her old aunt and uncle dancing with firewood around a large pot.

"What are you going to cook?" the girl asked.

"Come look!" the uncle said, laughing.

He took the lid off the pot as the girl looked in.

"It's just a root," the girl said, confused.

"Ha-ha!" the uncle gloated. "You don't recognize your little friend, do you? That is because we caught him when he was completely helpless! On the night when he must turn into a root!"

"It's the Ginseng Boy, and we're going to cook and eat it!" the aunt said. "And then your uncle and I will be young again!"

The girl began to cry, but the old people did not notice.

"I will be young again!" the uncle repeated, then stopped. *Eating part of the root will only make me younger,* he thought. *If I eat the whole thing, I would not only be young, but live forever too.*

The aunt didn't notice her husband's silence, for she was thinking the same thing. *Why share the root?* she thought. *I might only get a hundred more years. But if I eat all of it, I would never die.*

"Husband," the old woman said slyly, "the root must boil all day before we can eat it, and the water has not even warmed yet. Your parents live only an hour's walk west of here. Why don't you go and get them to share in our fortune? There'll be plenty for all."

"Dear wife," the man said. "I was just thinking the same about your parents! They are only an hour east of here. Why don't you go and get them?"

Slowly, both old people edged toward the door, each encouraging the other to leave. As the sun began to rise, they reluctantly parted ways, both constantly looking over their shoulders to check on each other.

Neither one, of course, gave a second thought to their little niece. However, as soon as they left the house, the girl wiped her eyes and stuck out her chin. She put out the fire and took the lid off the heavy pot. As the light of the sun streamed into the pot, the boy sat up and quickly jumped to the floor, dripping.

Just then, loud voices and the thumping of running footsteps were heard outside the door.

"Why are you rushing back?" the old man's voice said. "Where are your parents?"

"I wanted to make sure there was enough wood!" the woman said. "Where are your parents?"

"I wanted to make sure the door was locked!" the man said. "Let me help you with the wood!"

The door was flung open, and the old people and the children stared at one another.

"Quick!" the little girl said, and grabbing the boy's hand, they rushed past the aunt and uncle and out the door. With a scream, the woman swung a wooden log at them but instead hit her husband in the head. He, in turn, dropped his wood on her feet. Both fell to the ground, cradling their injured parts and cursing each other.

And what of their niece and the Ginseng Boy? They ran far, far away and were never heard from again.

"Thank you," Auntie Meiya said. She smiled again, but this time her smile was tired and her eyes dimmed.

"The little girl did her aunt and uncle a favor," Auntie Meiya said slowly, her eyes closing. "They would have been miserable immortals."

"Ah, but it's a difficult thing to refuse immortality," Amah said, beckoning to Yishan. He sat next to Meiya's bed and placed his hand in hers.

"It shouldn't be," Auntie Meiya said, her words even slower, as if she were speaking through water. With one last effort, she opened her eyes and looked at Yishan. "That kind of immortality is not for us humans. It would just drive us mad."

Auntie Meiya closed her eyes for the final time. Amah put her hand on Yishan's shoulder, and he bowed his head.

"Old woman!" the man said with impatience. "Did you hear me? Tell me the Story of the Ginseng Boy!"

Amah opened her eyes and looked into his face, startled again by the brutality in his black eyes.

"No," she said. Her heart beat as quickly as a battle drum, but she knew she had no other answer.

"No?" the man roared, his face so distorted with anger he looked more like an animal than a man, his teeth glittering in the flickering torchlight.

"No," Amah repeated. "You obviously already know it."

She watched him clench and unclench his fists, fighting the anger that wanted to explode inside him—an anger so intense that she knew he was rarely denied.

"You! You stupid old woman!" he finally sputtered. "I will deal with you later!"

He glared, shoved his helmet on his head, and stormed out of the tent. Amah stared at the forceful figure, powerful even as it disappeared into shadow.

"Until then," she whispered, "Your Exalted Majesty."

CHAPTER

12

Darkness was settling by the time they reached the bottom of the mountain, so Yishan suggested that they find shelter for the night in the village. Pinmei had not seen the village in a long time, but she knew it was not supposed to be as she was seeing it now. The silence of the street was cold, colder than the muffled quiet of winter. The few people there hardly glanced at them, and, slowly, Pinmei realized none of them smiled.

"No men," Yishan said, more to himself than to Pinmei. "Only women, children...and there's an old grandmother over there. Did Amah really know something? Why her?"

Of course, Pinmei thought, feeling foolish. The emperor had been through here. The wooden door of the house in front of her was smashed to pieces and the stones lying at her feet were from a destroyed wall. The silver-gray dust being thrown in the air by the wind was not snow, but ash.

"Excuse me," Yishan said to a woman sweeping up broken tiles. "We're from up the mountain, and we're on our way to the City of Bright Moonlight. Do you know where we could stay the night?"

The woman stared at them as if looking through thick ice. She shook her head and, without a word, went back into her house.

Yishan made the request again and again, and the response was the same each time. Even the young children, some of whom Pinmei recognized from her past visits, were strangely silent, gaping at them with hollowed eyes.

Finally, an old man spoke to them. "You had better come to my house," he said, sighing. "After the visit from the emperor's soldiers, no one else in this village has any hospitality left."

He led the way down the winding street to a humble stone

house, the grayed wooden door cracked and warped. A woman, her hair tightly knotted, stopped gluing paper on the broken windows to look at them.

"Children?" the woman said in dismay. "Old Sai, I send you for firewood and you come back with children?"

"We just want a place to sleep for the night," Yishan spoke quickly. "We aren't staying."

"A place is easy," the woman said with bitterness. "There are all the men's empty beds in this village. And empty horse stalls, pigpens, and chicken houses! The emperor's men took everything and left the villagers shells for their tears."

"Come, Suya," said Old Sai. "We are the luckiest people in the village right now. Could you have said that two days ago? This too may become a blessing."

The woman sighed again and waved them in, the ripped paper of the window flapping with more vigor than her hand. Pinmei and Yishan stepped through the doorway, the stone walls protecting them from the wind even as the cold seeped through the lattice windows.

"Auntie Suya! Old Sai!" a voice called from behind a plain wood screen. "Who's there?"

It was a man's voice. Curious, Pinmei and Yishan peeked around the screen. There, lying in bed, was a young man, obviously injured. As Pinmei came closer, she could see he was more of a boy than a man, perhaps only a handful of years older than Yishan.

"Hello," he said as he motioned them closer. His black eyes burned in the paleness of his face, and both of his legs were wrapped in bandages. But it was the tightness of his jaw that told of his constant pain.

"Did the soldiers do this to you?" Yishan asked.

"No," the man said, "though I have no doubt they could have easily. I watched them take Feng Fu, the mightiest man in the village. Feng swung an ax at a soldier, and it bounced right off the soldier's green sleeve as if it were a pebble hitting a turtle shell."

A soldier in green? Pinmei shivered and looked at Yishan, who was remembering his own encounter.

"I know that soldier," Yishan said. "He threw me with one hand as if I were a bug."

"He threw Feng Fu the same way," said the man, his eyes bulging at the memory. "With one hand. Huge Feng Fu! The man who strangled an ox with his bare hands! The emperor's soldiers must have special powers. They are invincible."

Soldiers, or just that soldier? Pinmei thought. She clasped Amah's bracelet, the cool stone warmer than her fingers.

"Well, if the emperor's soldiers didn't do this to you," said Yishan, nodding at the man's injuries, "who did?"

"My horse," the man said, and laughed.

"I don't see what's so funny about that," Yishan said.

"Well," the man said, "about a month ago, our mare ran away, and I cursed our bad luck until Old Sai said, 'You don't know. This may become a blessing.'"

"And I was right," Old Sai said, pulling up some chairs.

"Yes, you were," said the man. "Because a few weeks later, the horse returned—bringing back with it a splendid stallion. I was pleased with our good luck, but Old Sai said—"

"I said, 'You don't know. This may become a disaster,'" Old Sai finished, setting a small table close to the bed.

"And he was right," the man said. "Because a few days ago, when I was riding the stallion, it threw me and I broke both my legs. Again, I bemoaned my misfortune."

"And again," Old Sai said, sitting down, "I said, 'You don't know. This may become a blessing.'"

"And again you were right," Suya said, bringing in the tea. As she handed the young man his cup, she tenderly straightened his hair in a motherly gesture as she propped up his head. "For when the soldiers came, they rounded up all the men of the village. When they saw Sifen like this, they said he would be useless and left him."

"But all the other men were taken?" Yishan asked.

"All the other young men," Old Sai said, nodding. "They only wanted those who would be useful for work. They didn't take anyone old like me."

"Except for Amah," Pinmei said. Her voice had been faint, but they had still heard her. She felt their curious gazes as she whispered, "He took my grandmother."

A piece of tattered paper from the window blew into the room, floating for a moment between Pinmei and the others. It fell to the floor like a white flower petal.

"From the mountain," Old Sai said, slowly nodding. "Then, you are the Storyteller's granddaughter. I should have realized."

Storyteller, Pinmei thought. *That's what the soldier called Amah as well.* Her finger slowly circled the bracelet around her wrist, and she held it as close to herself as possible.

CHAPTER

13

"I hope you were not expecting dinner," the woman said. "We're poor people and we don't have food to spare."

"Suya," Sifen admonished. "These children are guests."

Suya flushed. "I'm sorry," she said. "I don't mean to be so stingy. It's just that the emperor's men seized everything. We would have nothing at all to eat if I hadn't managed to hide this."

With those words, Suya bent to the floor and pushed aside the blankets on Sifen's bed, revealing a wood plank on the floor. As she lifted the plank, Pinmei saw a stone had been removed from the floor to create a hiding space for a small jar. Everyone leaned in as Suya opened the jar and the uncooked rice began to fall from it like beads from a broken necklace.

"Oh!" Suya cried, and she quickly began to pick up the spilled rice. Pinmei knelt down to help her. Their eyes met and Pinmei felt a sudden kinship. She knew what it was like to be worried about rice in a jar.

"We can't afford to lose one grain now," Suya said to her. "After this is gone, we will have nothing."

"I wish I could give you the magic red stone," Pinmei said without thinking.

"Magic red stone?" Suya said.

"Oh, nothing," Pinmei said, her throat tightening. She felt her words begin to hide, as if scurrying to the hole in the floor.

"Too bad. It sounded like something from a story," Suya said with a wry smile. "We could use one. Sifen loves stories."

"Yes, I do!" Sifen said, overhearing their conversation. "Especially these days, when I would do anything to think of something other than this." He motioned to his bandaged legs and grimaced. "Come, Storyteller's granddaughter! Do you have a story to share?"

Pinmei opened her mouth, but no sound came out. A

stone of ice began to grow in her throat, and she clutched at the jade bracelet. How she wished Amah were here! Amah would tell these people a story; her safe, soothing voice would wrap them in a warm blanket. Pinmei felt a longing wash over her, and she shook her head.

"Yes, you do!" Yishan said in his scoffing tone. "Pinmei, you know every story Amah has ever told."

Pinmei felt everyone's eyes on her, and the stone in her throat grew and pushed against her lungs and heart. She tried to gulp, but the air seemed to have turned solid. *Amah!* Pinmei thought desperately. *I need you!* Blindly, she turned to run from the room in panic.

But a hot hand grabbed hers. Pinmei looked down to see Sifen gazing up at her, the lines on his face painting a picture of his pain.

"Please," he said. "Please, tell me a story."

The heat of his hand traveled up her arm, and the ice inside her began to melt. *Amah is not here*, Pinmei thought. *There's only me.* She looked again at Sifen's pleading eyes and swallowed. *When it is time for you to do something, you will do it.* Amah's words echoed, untying and smoothing the knotted string of Pinmei's voice. Slowly, Pinmei nodded. Then she took a deep breath, and, with a whisper, she started the story.

THE STORY OF THE RED STONE

After Nuwa, the goddess with the fish tail, mended the sky, there were still many problems. The sea overflowed with water from the Starry River of the Sky and churned with monstrous beasts. The waters were in complete chaos.

At that time, there was a young boy named Ku-Ang. His father had been a fisherman, so the sea's transformation was devastating to them. What had once been home was now a place of peril and the family was poverty stricken.

To help, Ku-Ang gathered firewood to sell to other villagers.

One day, while collecting wood, Ku-Ang saw something red glittering on the ground. Curious, he picked it up. It was a red stone.

It was small and round and smooth, and while it did not glow, it was so shiny Ku-Ang could see himself reflected in it.

It was rather pretty, so Ku-Ang thought he would give it to his mother. He put it in his lunch bag and continued to gather wood.

However, at lunchtime, there were two dumplings in his bag instead of one. Ku-Ang scratched his head. He was sure there had only been one dumpling in the morning. Had the stone done something?

When he returned home that evening, instead of giving the stone to his mother as he had planned, he slipped it into the half-empty rice jar.

The next morning, before his parents awoke, Ku-Ang peeked into the rice jar. The jar was full!

"It *was* the stone!" Ku-Ang said. Laughing, he called out to his family.

But after Ku-Ang told his story, his father shook his head.

"That stone does not belong to us," he said. "You must return it to where you found it."

Ashamed, Ku-Ang returned to the mountain forest. When he arrived at the place where he had found the stone, he saw an old man sitting as if waiting for him.

"Was this your stone?" Ku-Ang asked as he bowed and offered the stone.

"There are three things of Nuwa left here on earth," the old man said, ignoring Ku-Ang's question. "A tear, a strand of hair, and a drop of blood. You are holding the drop of blood."

Ku-Ang gasped and dropped the red stone in the old man's lap. The old man looked into Ku-Ang's eyes.

"If you are pure of heart," the old man said, "this stone will bring the Sea King to calm the waters."

The Sea King? Ku-Ang's eyes widened. If the Sea King could calm the waters, the monsters would stop coming to shore. People would not live in fear and his father could fish again. The world could return to normal.

"But to find him," the old man said, placing the stone back in Ku-Ang's hand, "you must bring the stone safely to the top of the mountain north of the village."

Ku-Ang gulped. No one went to the Northern Mountain. Evil beasts plagued the way. But to have a Sea King! Ku-Ang turned and began to make his way to the Northern Mountain.

To get to the Northern Mountain, Ku-Ang had to cross the abandoned Black Bridge. As he stepped onto it, a monstrous snake sprang from the water, and Ku-Ang saw horrible, sharp teeth coming toward him. But right before they snapped upon him, the snake caught sight of Ku-Ang's prize.

"The red stone!" it hissed. "You wish to go to the Northern Mountain?"

"Yes," Ku-Ang said, his head high even though his legs trembled.

"Do you know horrible Haiyi?" the evil creature asked.

Horrible Haiyi? He was the wicked bully of the village. Ku-Ang knew Haiyi and his cruelty all too well.

"Yes." Ku-Ang nodded.

"I will let you pass if you agree to bring me the ears of horrible Haiyi's old mother," the enormous snake hissed. "Or I will kill you right now!"

"Never!" Ku-Ang shouted instantly. "I have my own mother, and I will never harm another's!"

"Then die!" the snake hissed, and it seized Ku-Ang with its knifelike teeth, lifted him up into the sky, and flung him away with all its might.

Ku-Ang landed painfully on the ground, across the lake, bleeding and gasping. But the stone was still in his hand, so he pushed himself up and began to stagger toward the Northern Mountain. He had only made it halfway across the plain when a large black shadow began to circle around him. Clutching his injured side, he looked up.

Above him was a gigantic, vile bird, green poison shining on its feathers. With a horrible shriek, it landed in front of Ku-Ang, its foul smell making him flinch.

"The red stone!" it screeched. "You wish to go to the Northern Mountain?"

"Yes," Ku-Ang said.

"Do you know horrible Haiyi?" the bird screamed.

Ku-Ang nodded.

"I will let you pass if you agree to bring me the bones of horrible Haiyi's younger brother," the evil bird screeched. "Or I will kill you now."

"Never!" Ku-Ang shouted. "I have my own brother, and I would never harm another's!"

"Then die!" the bird shrieked, and it grabbed Ku-Ang with its stabbing claws, flew into the sky, and flung him away with all its might.

When Ku-Ang was finally able to open his eyes and sit up, he saw he sat on the Northern Mountain.

The sea stretched below him, the red stone was in his hand, and the top of the mountain was not far away. Although he sobbed with pain, he knew he could not give up now. Swaying and stumbling, he made his way toward the top of the mountain.

Just as he was reaching the top, he heard a loud shout that filled him with dread. It was horrible Haiyi!

"Ku-Ang!" Haiyi bellowed. "Give me that stone!"

Ku-Ang clutched the stone. He could not let Haiyi have it. Should he throw it into the sea? *But then I'll never find the Sea King*, Ku-Ang thought. "What should I do?"

The ruffian had almost reached him. His ugly face jeered as he saw that Ku-Ang was trapped. "Give me that stone," Haiyi called, "or I'll get you!"

"Never!" Ku-Ang shouted, and he put the stone in his mouth and swallowed it.

Immediately, an excruciating pain burned inside him. A noise bellowed from his throat, startling Haiyi and himself. Ku-Ang fell backward off the cliff, slowly turning and spinning in the air.

The sky seemed to embrace him, for the wind blew around him as if coating him with a new skin. The pain from the stone began to dissipate, but Ku-Ang could still feel its power pulsating; his whole body felt as if it were bursting.

Ku-Ang stretched his hands in front of him, and, with shock, he saw they had turned into claws! His arms were covered in scales! And as he plummeted downward, he saw his reflection in the strangely still water. He had turned into a dragon!

The sea stirred. A wild whirlpool began to spin, its white waves becoming a herd of *longma*—dragon horses—racing to herald him in. When Ku-Ang touched the water, a crashing roar echoed and the entire sea opened, as if welcoming an honored ruler.

For it was. Ku-Ang, the Sea King, had arrived.

"So the boy turned into a dragon and found himself the king of the sea," Old Sai said.

Pinmei looked at him in surprise, her eyes refocusing. She had gotten so lost in telling the story she had forgotten people were listening.

"That was great!" Sifen said, his face glowing. "You truly are the Storyteller's granddaughter!" And Pinmei felt a shy smile creep onto her face.

"That red stone," Yishan said. "I know we're not sure

about the dragon's pearl...Do you think maybe that's the stone the emperor is looking for?" He looked at her.

Pinmei slowly shook her head. "The red stone never glowed," Pinmei said. "It would never have lit the night like the one the emperor keeps asking for."

"And what would the emperor want with a stone that doubles rice and dumplings? He has plenty of both!" Suya said, but she was looking at Sifen's changed face with a smile. She turned to include the others, and Pinmei saw that unlike her earlier close-lipped smile, this one was soft and kind.

"Maybe the emperor would want it so he could be transformed into a dragon," Old Sai suggested.

"I doubt it," Sifen said. "Besides, didn't the old man say you had to be pure of heart? You couldn't say that about the emperor."

"Shh! Sifen!" Suya said, looking as if she were afraid a soldier would jump out of a wall. She stood up and shook her head. "I'll go start dinner," she said, and then added, with a warm glance at the children, "for all of us."

CHAPTER

14

Amah fell on the stone floor of the dungeon. The guard said nothing but lifted her so she sat against the wall and locked a long leg chain around her ankle. Then, as if ashamed, he took off his outer garment and laid it over her. Feeling its warmth on her, Amah looked up at him gratefully, but he did not meet her eyes. Instead, he turned and closed the door.

"Ah, another lucky one," a weak voice said.

Amah turned toward the voice, her eyes adjusting to the dim light. A man sat on the opposite side like a stick of bamboo leaning against the wall, his leg also chained.

"Are we lucky?" Amah said.

"Yes," the man said. "We are prisoners. It is obvious the emperor does not keep many. He prefers to send them to work or have them killed."

Amah looked at him, noticing the whiteness of his skin and his gaunt face.

"You have been a prisoner a long time," she said.

"I was imprisoned by the emperor when he was still known as the Tiger King," the man said with a bitter laugh. "While the Imperial Palace is supposed to be grander, the dungeons are all the same."

"The emperor took you with him?" Amah asked.

"Strange, is it not?" the man said. "But he thinks he might have need for me in the future. He said as much when he had the guards take me away. First he ordered me executed, but then he changed his mind."

"Changed his mind?" Amah said. "Why were you being punished to begin with?"

"Well," the man said, "a giant white stone washed up from the sea and the Tiger King ordered me to make a sculpture of himself on a horse from it."

"And you didn't?" Amah said.

"Oh, I did," the stonecutter said. "My daughter and I worked on it for months. But when we finished, my daughter said, 'Father, the horse is so beautiful, but the man is so ugly! He ruins it!' And I could not help but agree. Finally, we could not bear it, so my daughter and I smashed the man off the horse. Of course, the Tiger King was not happy."

"So he was going to have you executed." Amah nodded. "Then what happened?"

"I remember it well," the man said, as if in a dream. "The guards were just about to drag me away when the Tiger King said under his breath, 'He said I would not learn from my mistakes. Bah!' And then he ordered the guards to stop and said, 'Put him in the dungeon. I may have need for him later.'"

"Ah, I see." Amah nodded again. "How interesting. The past repeats itself."

"The past?" the stonecutter said, looking at Amah. "You know of another stonecutter who shared my fate?"

"Almost," Amah said. "The story is very similar."

"Tell me," the stonecutter said.

THE STORY OF THE STONE FISH

L
ong ago, a strange stone from the sea rolled up onto the shore. It was smooth, pure white, and the width of a *gang* of wine. The townspeople were sure it was lucky—perhaps even a gift from the Sea King himself. Finally, word of the stone came to the ears of the magistrate of the town.

The magistrate was well known for his ruthlessness, as well as his greed. He was powerful, so powerful! The magistrate was said to have the ear of the emperor's most trusted advisor, and his own son was king of a neighboring city. As a result, he ruled his area with absolute power, roaring his orders so constantly the villagers called him Magistrate Tiger.

When Magistrate Tiger roared for the stone, his subjects brought it without delay. The magistrate marveled at the stone's beauty. Immediately he called in the most skilled stonecutter in the village.

"Carve me a dragon from this stone," the magistrate ordered. "An immortal dragon of power cut from this stone will be a fitting sculpture for my formal chamber."

A dragon! The stonecutter gulped. Only the imperial family was allowed to use an image of a dragon. The magistrate's imperial connection was only by his son's marriage—not considered strong enough to claim a dragon! But he knew better than to protest, so he nodded and took the stone to carve.

As he carried the stone, it seemed to wriggle and squirm in his arms. *"Bubble...bubble...glub...glub..."* the stone seemed to whisper to him. "Shh," the stonecutter whispered back. "You are to be a dragon."

However, when the stonecutter began to carve, the head that formed was not a dragon's. The carved eyes gazed at him with such a reproachful stare that the stonecutter set down his tools.

His young son, who often helped him with his work, stood next to the stonecutter in silence.

"Baba," the stonecutter's son said finally, "that stone does not want to be a dragon. It wants to be a fish."

The stonecutter nodded, but his head hung with heaviness. He could not carve a dragon from this stone. But Magistrate Tiger...

"Glub, glub," the stone said, and when the stonecutter

raised his head to look at the stone, he saw the beseeching eyes of a trapped creature.

"Poor fish!" the son said. "Baba, it wants to be free!"

The stonecutter knew he could not ignore the stone's plea. He sighed and began to carve.

Ninety-nine days later, the magistrate came to collect his dragon and, instead, found a stone fish. The fish glistened as if it had just jumped out of the water, its every scale carved with such delicacy they seemed transparent. It was a masterpiece.

Of course, that did not matter to the magistrate. He was furious to be presented with a fish when he had commanded a dragon. He ordered the stonecutter to be taken away and executed.

That night, the magistrate could not sleep. "*Bubble, bubble, bubble,*" something kept whispering to him. "*Glub, glub.*"

The fish! the magistrate thought. In the morning, he ordered that the fish carving be brought to him.

The stonecutter's son brought it. Knowing he was carrying his father's last masterpiece, the stonecutter's son could not help but begin to weep. But just as his salty tears touched the stone, the fish began to wriggle and twist.

"*Glub, glub!*" said the fish. It was alive!

"Quickly!" Magistrate Tiger roared. "Water!"

Immediately, the servants brought a wood tub filled with water from the kitchen. The stonecutter's son released the fish, and it began to swim.

How amazing it was! Its every curve was an iridescent medley of color. Its every movement was a joyful dance. It flipped and splashed with such delight that even the selfish magistrate smiled. All who saw the fish could not help but feel happy, if only for that brief moment.

The magistrate was extremely proud. His magical stone fish was talked and whispered about everywhere. His people tried to catch glimpses of it. His flattering assistants fawned over it. His noble friends admired it. There was even talk that the emperor himself was interested in seeing it. "The happy fish," they murmured. "Have you seen it? Magistrate Tiger has a marvel!"

"It is too bad the fish swims in such a humble home," one of the magistrate's assistants said. "A wooden kitchen tub does not seem fitting for a creature."

"Yes," Magistrate Tiger said, struck by the thought. "You are right. Have the finest *gang* brought here. The fish shall have a new home."

Soon, a decorated *gang* was brought to the magistrate's chamber and filled with water. But as the servant lifted the fish, it writhed and twisted, jumping out of the servant's hands.

Crack! The fish lay lifeless on the floor—now broken pieces of stone.

The magistrate held the stone parts in his hands and tried to fit them together. "My fish!" he cried. "My fish! Get the stonecutter to come fix it!"

The others stared and gulped. "We cannot," one said finally. "You had the stonecutter put to death. And there is no one else skilled enough to mend it."

The magistrate was silent for a moment, realizing the truth of his assistant's words. He gave a roar of rage, perhaps cursing himself for his own lack of vision.

"Ah! But the stonecutter did not die!" the prisoner said. "His son did not know it at the time, but he was able to get away, and later they both fled the magistrate's land together!"

"Did they?" Amah said.

"Yes, yes," the prisoner said with pride. "I know this because that stonecutter was my ancestor! He passed his skill down from generation to generation to..." The man broke off and looked closely at Amah. His face broke out in a wide smile.

"I know who you are!" he said, almost with glee. "There is only one person other than my own grandmother who would know that story and could have told it the way you did. You must be the Storyteller!"

"I have been called that," Amah admitted.

"Ah! I truly am a lucky one after all," the stonecutter said. "For to be in prison with the Storyteller is to not be in a prison at all."

CHAPTER
15

"I feel I shouldn't let you leave," Suya said, shaking her head. The cold morning light cascaded through the window. Pinmei and Yishan were packed to go. They had planned to leave before breakfast so as not to add to Suya's food worries, but she pushed two bowls of hot porridge into their hands. "Children, walking alone to the City of Bright Moonlight! In winter? You're meeting someone there?"

Yishan nodded. "Well, I'm sure we will meet someone," he hissed at Pinmei when he caught her guilty expression. Pinmei could easily imagine Suya's horror if she knew the truth.

"Sifen, Old Sai!" Suya said, shaking her head again. "Tell them to stay!"

"I wish I could go with you," Sifen said from his bed, the longing obvious in his voice.

Old Sai brought them two rolls. "A leather ground cover and two fur blankets," he said with satisfaction. His eyes twinkled at them. "From the hidden hole under my bed!"

"We'll bring them back," Pinmei said, realizing their value.

"Just bring back a good tale, Storyteller's granddaughter," Old Sai said kindly.

"Yes," Sifen called, "I'll be expecting a good one!"

And with that, they left. The door of the stone house closed and the silence of winter mocked them. Suddenly, Pinmei yearned for the sound of Amah's voice, and, inside, she felt as if the ever-present hollow ache would swallow her. She blinked her eyes at the glittering ice-covered stones and took a deep breath. It was time to leave the mountain.

Yishan lead Pinmei to the main road as she nestled into her multicolored coat, its warmth like Amah's arms.

The snow began to fall—gently at first, but then heavier and heavier, flakes dropping and fluttering all around. *They're like white butterflies*, Pinmei thought, *hundreds and hundreds of white butterflies—and one red one?* A wavering, brilliant red color flittered in front of her. *A red butterfly! Impossible!* Pinmei shook her head, and when she looked again, there was only the white falling snow. She must be seeing things.

After a good distance, the grumbling in Yishan's stomach became so loud he had to admit he was hungry. As they unrolled the leather ground cover to sit at the side of the road, they found a package with a generous supply of rice balls, most likely smuggled in by Sifen or Old Sai. With cries of delight, they fell upon them as if they were candied berries.

"I hope they don't get in trouble with Suya for giving us these," said Pinmei with appreciation. Yishan grunted in agreement, his mouth too full to reply, and for a moment all was quiet except for their satisfied munching.

But only for a moment. For just as Pinmei swallowed her second rice ball, there was a faint rumble in the distance. She recognized that sound. *Horses!* Pinmei looked at Yishan in alarm.

He had cocked his head, listening intently. "Just one horse," he said, "and coming fast. He probably won't even notice us."

Pinmei listened again. She could hear the galloping hooves on the stone now. They waited, not even attempting to swallow their food. Faster and closer, faster and closer, faster and closer, and at last, like a cresting wave, the rider burst out of the silver mist.

As the rider passed, Pinmei gaped at him. He was riding a milk-white horse, so white the animal blended into the snow. The rider, a flash of gleaming blue silk, looked like he was flying. They passed only for a moment, but the horse's thundering hooves belied its grace, for it seemed to glide more than run.

As the horse and rider began to fade into the distance, Pinmei kept staring, unable to look away. So she saw it clearly when the horse screamed with a panicked shriek and reared, and the blue smear of the thrown rider collapsed to the ground.

CHAPTER
16

Both Pinmei and Yishan ran to the rider. The horse had melted into the white landscape, but the mound of luxurious gray-and-blue silk on the ground reassured them that it had not been a dream. Yishan gently turned the rider over, and they both gasped. The rider was a woman!

And she was a stunningly beautiful woman. Only moments before, Pinmei had decided the horse was the pinnacle of beauty, but now she found herself reconsidering. The opulent fur-trimmed silk and gold ornaments told of the woman's wealth and nobility, but those were mere faded trappings compared with her loveliness. Her face, so pure and clear, could have been formed of water jade and her shining hair, loosened from its ornate pins, pooled around her like smooth black water on the white snow. Even Yishan looked amazed.

The woman opened her eyes.

"Children?" she murmured. "Why are there children here? What has happened?"

"Your horse threw you," Yishan said. "We wanted to make sure you were all right."

The woman sat up. She looked at them and at the countryside around her. Pinmei noticed that her eyes looked as if happiness had not shone in them for a long time.

"I remember now," the woman said, her voice like a bamboo water chime. "BaiMa reared suddenly. It's not like him at all. Something unexpected must have surprised him."

Pinmei remembered the red butterfly she thought she had seen in the snow. Could that have surprised the horse?

"Do I still have..." The woman pushed aside her folds of silk and held a small bag up to her chest. She breathed a sigh of relief. "Here it is. I hope it was not hurt."

The woman opened the bag and pulled out a lavishly embroidered fabric. As she held it open, Pinmei found herself gawking. It was an embroidered picture. There was a grand mansion surrounded by a beautiful garden with flowered fishponds and red-pillared pavilions. A sparkling river flowed before a stone wall, and mountains disappeared into a sea of clouds. The finest details were included, from the butterfly-shaped windows to the swimming ducks. Pinmei knew Amah was known for her embroidery skills, but this was extraordinary. Every thread vibrated with color.

"How beautiful," Pinmei breathed, her awe overcoming her shyness. "It's just like the widow's embroidery in Amah's story."

"Story?" the woman inquired.

"Oh, everything reminds her of a story," Yishan said mockingly, but also with a touch of pride. "Pinmei is a storyteller."

I am? Pinmei thought with surprise. She had thought herself many things before—a scared mouse, a quiet girl, a coward—but never a storyteller. But before she could think further, the woman gave her a smile.

"Well, I'm not sure if I am ready to get up yet," the woman said. "So perhaps a story would be good medicine."

Pinmei began to shake her head in protest, but the woman's eyes were weighted with so much worry that Pinmei found her own heart pale. The green of the jade bracelet shimmered at her, like a thread in one Amah's embroidery silks. Again Pinmei felt the familiar longing pierce her. Amah would never refuse to tell a story—how could she? So, with her voice slightly trembling, Pinmei began.

THE STORY OF THE WIDOW'S EMBROIDERY

There was once a widow who was extremely skilled at embroidery. When she embroidered a flower, bees would try to nestle in it. When she embroidered a tree, birds would try to land on it. She was known far and wide and supported herself and her young son with the embroidered pieces she sold.

One day, when she was at the market, she saw an old man selling a painting of a palatial estate. There was an elegant villa with lakes dotted with orange fish and moon gates that led to courtyards lined with trees. She stared at the painting, and a yearning she had never felt before filled her. Without thinking, she spent all the money meant for rice and bought the painting.

When she returned home, she showed the painting to her son.

"If only we could live in this painting," she said to him with tears in her eyes. "I feel as if my heart will break if I do not live in this place."

"Well, Mother," the son said, trying to comfort her, "your embroidery is so lifelike perhaps you should embroider this picture. Then you will feel the same as if you were living in it."

The widow's face lit up and she nodded. "Yes, of course," she said, and immediately went to work.

And she did not stop working. Hour after hour her needle moved, and at night she lit a lantern to continue. She carried on like this for days, and the days turned into months. Her son, without complaint, began to cut wood to support them.

The months turned into years. The widow's hair turned white, and when strands fell from her head, she embroidered them into clouds. Her needle pricked her fingers, and when her blood dripped, she stitched it into the red peonies. They could no longer afford lantern oil, so she burned branches, and when her eyes watered from the smoke, she sewed her tears into the lotus ponds.

Finally, after eight years, the old widow put down her needle. She was finished. Her son, who was now a young man, stood in awe as he looked at the completed piece. It was magnificent. The widow sighed a soft sound of contentment.

The door banged open, and a wild wind burst into the room. The embroidery flew into the air and out the door. The widow and her son rushed after it, but only saw it fluttering in the distance. The widow collapsed to the ground.

When the widow finally opened her eyes, she begged her son to find her embroidery. "I shall die without it," she said.

So the son left his mother in the care of his neighbors and went in search of the embroidery. After many days of traveling, he found himself by the sea. The moon was rising and its reflection on the water made a long silver-white path that connected seamlessly with the ground. As the young man followed the moon path with his eyes, he was startled to see a small figure lying on the shore. It was a boy.

"Hello!" the boy said as he fixed his red cap. "What are you doing here?"

The widow's son then saw this was not an ordinary young boy. *He must be an immortal of some sort,* the son thought. So he told the boy his story.

"Oh, that embroidery," the boy said. "The Sea King's daughter sent a servant for it. She and all her ladies in waiting are copying it for their own pieces."

"I must get it back," the son said. "My mother will die without it."

"You'd have to go to the Sea King's palace, and that's a hard journey," the boy said. "First you must swim the sea until you reach frozen water and dive into it without a shiver or moan. If you make one sound of discontent, you will turn into ice and shatter into ten thousand pieces. Do you still want to go?"

The son nodded and started immediately to walk to the ocean. The boy grabbed his arm.

"Wait!" the boy said. "I'll get you a ride."

The boy put two fingers in his mouth and made a shrill whistle. The waves of the sea roared, and as the water rolled off the shore, a huge white stone appeared. The boy went over to the stone and knocked on it.

"Come out!" he said. "This fellow needs a ride!"

Did the stone quiver? The widow's son rubbed his eyes.

"Hurry up!" the boy said. "She'll never even notice you're gone. She's busy sewing. Come on!"

The waves smashed into the stone and made a crackling noise like a porcelain plate breaking. When the water withdrew, a white horse stood among some broken pieces of matching white stone.

"Good," the boy said. "He's in a hurry."

The boy made a motion with his hand, and the horse walked up to the son.

"Now you'll make it," the boy said with a grin.

The widow's son, after closing his gaping mouth, nodded his thanks, climbed on the horse's back, and galloped into the water.

The horse and the young man swam through the piercing cold water. The dark waves flung shards of ice at him, and the blood from his cuts steamed and froze. When the water no longer churned and all was silent, the horse plunged into the bitter water and all was black.

When the son opened his eyes, he was warm and dry and still on the horse. The sun was overhead, and a majestic palace of crystal was before him. Without his urging, the horse entered the palace and brought him to a grand hall, where his mother's embroidery hung in a place of honor. Dozens of beautiful women were sitting around it, each sewing a copy.

"I'm here for my mother's embroidery," he announced.

The women looked at him and whispered to one another until one, dressed in blue and the loveliest of them all, rose. It was only then that he saw she had a fish tail instead of legs. "Let us keep it for the rest of today so we can finish our copies," she said. "You may take it tomorrow."

The widow's son was awestruck by her beauty. Even with her fish tail, she was the most stunning creature he had ever encountered, and he, who had not been turned by pain or possible death, found he could not refuse her. So he let himself be led to a golden bed at the back of the hall, where he soon fell asleep.

In the meantime, the women rushed to finish their pieces. They called their servants to bring more threads and silks, and the woman in blue requested a new needle. "Fetch the finest one we have from my father's treasury," she ordered her servant.

But one by one, each woman rose to compare her work with the original, shook her head in defeat, and abandoned the hall.

The last one to leave was the woman with the fish tail. She, of course, was the Sea King's daughter—the most beautiful as well as the most skilled. But as she held her embroidery up to the widow's, she too shook her head. Hers, like the others, was a poor copy. No one could match the fineness or colors of the widow's silver clouds, flaming flowers, or crystal lakes. *The widow's embroidery is so beautiful*, the Sea King's daughter thought with yearning. *I love it so. I wish I could be a part of it.*

And with that whim, she began to embroider a small image of herself in the garden of the widow's embroidery. *But I'll give myself legs*, she thought with an amused smile, *because it's a picture of a mortal land.* When she finished, it was late and she was quite tired. She tucked her needle into the widow's embroidery to retrieve in the morning and left for bed.

When the son woke up, it was still dark and the hall was empty. His mother's embroidery still hung at the front of the room, glistening in the fading moonlight. *What if the Sea Daughter and her ladies change their minds?* he thought. *I'd better go now.*

So he took the embroidery as quietly as possible and jumped onto the waiting horse. The amazing horse took off at a gallop, racing up through the water, across the frozen sea, and back to the seaside.

When they reached the shore, the man dismounted. The horse waded into the water and an ocean wave washed over it. When the water withdrew, the horse was, again, a large white stone. Then, another large crest rose and scooped the stone back to the sea.

The young man gazed at the empty impression on the shore and at the rolled embroidery in his hand. Without another pause, he turned and ran home.

"Mother!" he called as he burst into the house. The widow was in bed, thin and pale, with her eyes closed, and he feared the worst. He rushed to her side and laid the embroidery on her. "Your embroidery is here. I have returned."

Slowly, the widow's fingers touched the smooth, delicate threads. Her eyes opened and she smiled, her second smile in over eight years.

"My son," she said with one hand on the embroidery and the other clasping his, "help me bring this out in the light so I may see it better."

Outside, they carefully spread the embroidery on the ground. As they unfolded it, the silk grew and grew. It covered their poor house and bare land, and in its place, the stately manor and a glorious garden formed. The widow's embroidery was coming to life! The swimming fish in the sparkling water, the trees with the jade-green leaves, the courtyard with patterned walkways—all real!

Everything was exactly as the widow had sewed it, except for one thing. For standing among the brilliant flowers and fluttering butterflies was a beautiful woman dressed in blue. She held a silver needle in her fingers and was looking around in confusion, for it was the Sea King's daughter who had sewn herself into the embroidery.

But when she saw the widow and the son, her expression cleared and was replaced with one of affection. She saw she could not love the embroidery so much without loving its creator and her son.

The delighted widow welcomed her to share in her incredible fortune. The son and the Sea King's daughter soon married, and the widow lived the rest of her days in complete contentment.

"Is that the end?" the noblewoman asked in an almost-demanding tone. "What else happened to the son and the Sea King's daughter?"

"I suppose," Pinmei said, a little surprised, "after they were married, they lived happily as well."

"Yes, but..." The woman stopped midsentence, and both Pinmei and Yishan looked toward where she was staring. A glimmer of scarlet was wavering in the white-and-gray sky. The red butterfly! Pinmei hadn't imagined it!

The two children and the woman watched without moving. The butterfly flittered through the falling snowflakes. Back and forth, back and forth it went, an intricate, silent dance.

At last, the butterfly landed on the noblewoman's lap, on top of the gorgeous embroidery. It gave one final tremble and vanished.

Pinmei blinked her eyes. Had the butterfly melted into the embroidery? Or had a gust of wind blown it away? Where did it go?

But then the woman gave a low cry of anguish, so full of sorrow and heartache all other thoughts disappeared.

"He is dead," the woman whispered, and a single tear began to roll down her cheek.

CHAPTER
17

"Who is dead?" Yishan asked, handing her his handkerchief.

The woman wiped her tear and closed her eyes as if she could not bear to see land around her. After a moment, she raised her head.

"My husband," she said softly. "I am Lady Meng, and my husband has been away on the king's business for more than a year. Four days ago, I had an overwhelming feeling something terrible had happened, and finally, I could not stand it. I was on my way to the City of Bright Moonlight to find out when BaiMa threw me."

Snowflakes dropped onto the embroidery, but Lady Meng did not bother to brush them away. Instead, her fingers stroked the smooth threads of a crimson butterfly Pinmei hadn't noticed before.

"I knew when he left he was in danger," the woman continued. She was looking out into the empty sky, and Pinmei knew she had forgotten about them. "I sewed him a dragon shirt to protect him, leaving in my needle, but even then I knew it would not be enough. He laughed and said he would return to me with the flight of the first butterfly…"

Her words dripped into the cold air, and while she seemed awash in sadness, she did not shed another tear. Instead, as if suddenly waking, she looked at them.

"Well, my young friends, Pinmei and…" Lady Meng looked sharply at Yishan as if trying to remember him. He gazed back at her, his face as blank as uncarved stone.

"Yishan," Pinmei said, slightly confused.

Lady Meng smiled and returned the handkerchief. "Where are you going and why?" she asked.

"We're going to the City of Bright Moonlight too," Yishan said, and told Lady Meng the reason for their travels.

"For the dragon's pearl," Lady Meng said after Yishan had finished, "you'll have to see King KaeJae. He is the king of the City of Bright Moonlight. It was he who asked my husband for help."

"What did he need help with?" Yishan asked.

"King KaeJae knew the old emperor would soon be overthrown," Lady Meng said, "and a new emperor would come to power. New emperors usually execute all the old kings and replace them. King KaeJae wanted my husband's advice so he and the city could survive."

"The king must have trusted your husband a lot," Yishan said.

"Yes, they were good friends," Lady Meng said. "That is why I have questions for him."

"What will you ask him?" Yishan said. Pinmei continued to marvel at his boldness. *He could be talking to a farmer or an emperor*, Pinmei thought, remembering Yishan's unbowed head the night the hut burned, *and it wouldn't matter*.

However, while Lady Meng's eyes flashed with sudden anger, it was not from Yishan's impertinence. "I want to know how my husband died," she said.

"Will it make a difference?" Yishan asked with surprising gentleness.

Lady Meng flushed and bowed her head. "Perhaps not," she said softly. "But I still need to know."

Pinmei looked at Lady Meng, shimmering with finery like a queen. To get the dragon's pearl, they would have to ask to see the king, which, Pinmei suspected, would result in mocking laughter. Lady Meng, however, would be invited in immediately. Maybe Lady Meng could bring them! Should she ask? No, she wouldn't dare! But Amah's bracelet gently pressed on Pinmei's wrist with the weight of a loving hand. Pinmei took a deep breath.

"Um, maybe, since we all, um, need to see the king," Pinmei said hesitantly, "maybe we could all go together..."

Pinmei's face flushed to the same color as Yishan's hat.

"That is a good idea," Lady Meng said. "BaiMa can bring us."

"Your horse?" Yishan said. "But he ran—"

A nicker sounded, and Yishan and Pinmei swung around. There, like a white jade statue in the snow mist, was BaiMa, Lady Meng's horse.

CHAPTER

18

"But don't you want to go ahead to the city on BaiMa?" asked Yishan. "We will just slow you down."

"There is no rush for me now," Lady Meng said, sorrow splashing across her face again. "We will travel together. BaiMa can carry us."

"All three of us?" Yishan asked. "That is a lot for a horse."

"Pinmei is little more than a mouse," Lady Meng said with a smile, "and BaiMa is a special horse."

And she was right. BaiMa was even more majestic and larger than Pinmei remembered. His sinewy, broad back was more like a dragon's than a horse's, and he had enough strength to carry a legion of men. As they rode, the empty sky and snow melted into each other, making Pinmei feel as if they were sailing on a vast white sea. When they finally reached the Jade River, the road broke off in four directions. Both Yishan and Lady Meng looked at the roads with dismay.

"Do you know which road to take?" Lady Meng said. "They all look the same in the winter."

"There should be a marker," Yishan said, jumping off BaiMa to dig through a pile of snow.

After some searching, they found the stone marker—or what remained of it—buried in snow. It had fallen to the ground, because of either the wind or vandals, and broken to pieces. What to do? The barren landscape made all the snow-covered roads look the same. In fact, if it were not for the Jade River in front of her, Pinmei would not even know which road they had already traveled on.

And it was the frozen Jade River that Lady Meng was staring at. Instead of looking from road to road, like Pinmei and Yishan were, Lady Meng's eyes were fixed on the ice stretching before them like a silver brocade.

Finally, Lady Meng turned around and reached into

the saddlebags. "Yishan," she said, "come with me to break the ice."

Pinmei threw Yishan a questioning glance, but he only reached down to grab a shard of broken stone and they both followed Lady Meng toward the river.

The ice was solid under their feet, but as they walked farther, Pinmei could hear the faint whispers of water growing louder. Just as Pinmei was starting to worry that the ice might be thinning, Lady Meng stopped.

"Break the ice here, Yishan," she directed.

Yishan grinned, knelt down, and struck the ice with his stone. *Whack!* Immediately, the ice cracked, and a gash of dark water, like black ink, trembled in anxious waves.

From her sleeve, Lady Meng pulled out a set of gold chopsticks and dipped them into the water as if fishing for a dumpling in soup.

"Ah!" Lady Meng said with triumph. She waved her chopsticks. They were holding a smooth dark stone.

No, it wasn't a stone, Pinmei realized as she looked closer. It was a shell. Lady Meng was holding a mussel.

"Show us the way to the City of Bright Moonlight," Lady Meng commanded the mussel.

Pinmei sneaked a look at Yishan. What was Lady Meng trying to do?

"Show us the way to the City of Bright Moonlight," she said again, louder and slower.

The mussel did nothing.

"Lazy thing," Lady Meng sighed. She flung the shell into the air. "Wake up! Show us the way to the City of Bright Moonlight!"

And as the mussel spun into the sky, it burst into feathers. It was a bird! It hung above them, its chest a stitch of red thread in the white silk sky.

"A swallow!" Pinmei breathed. "The mussel turned into a swallow!"

Lady Meng had already turned back toward the road and Yishan trailed comically behind, his mouth open and head angled upward. But Pinmei stood still, curiously studying Lady Meng, who, against the whiteness of snow and ice, looked like a painting come to life.

CHAPTER
19

The dungeon was cold, but not bitterly so. The thick earthen walls protected the prisoners from freezing, but the only light was the single torch left by the guard. Amah was not sure if days or weeks had passed.

"I have heard many stories about you, you know," the stonecutter said. He gave a restrained chuckle. "Stories about the Storyteller! Strange, is it not?"

"What have you heard?" Amah asked.

"Many things," the stonecutter said, "and each more marvelous than the other. They say you carried a dragon's pearl to your parents in your youth and later predicted the destruction of the first Capital City. They say you know immortals and dragons!"

"Every time a story is told, it changes," Amah said. "Stories about myself are no different."

"I was told you were honored by kings, and even invited to reside at the Imperial Palace, but you refused," the stonecutter continued. "Instead you chose to live in complete seclusion on Never-Ending Mountain."

"Not in seclusion," Amah objected. "I have a grand-daughter."

"Ah," the stonecutter said, a glint of mischief flashing through his lopsided smile. "Then all the rest is true?"

Amah laughed, suddenly appreciating the character of her companion.

"Let me tell you a story," she said.

THE STORY OF THE
PAINTED LION EYES

There was a girl who had a dragon for a friend. They loved each other dearly, so it was with great sadness when, one day, the dragon told her they must part.

"I've been given a mandate from heaven," he told her. "I will be helping the Blue Dragon bring in spring. It is a great honor. But once I begin, I cannot be seen by mortal eyes. We will never meet again."

The girl tried to smile at her friend's good fortune, but she could not hide her dismay.

"I always meant to watch over you," the dragon said sadly, "but now I cannot. So I looked at your future in the Book of Fortune."

"You should not have done that," the girl gasped.

"I had to," the dragon said. "I could not leave without knowing your future."

"Don't tell me!" the girl said, raising her hands to cover her ears. "I should not know!"

The dragon gently lowered the girl's hands with his claw.

"I must tell you this," the dragon said. "There will be a day when you will experience the greatest joy and the greatest sadness of your life at the same time. When that happens, you must watch the stone lions of your city. When the eyes of the stone lions turn red, you must take a boat to the closest island. There, you will find the Iron Rod."

"The Iron Rod?" the girl said. "But it's at Sea Bottom! To help keep the waters steady."

"Don't worry," the dragon said. "I have already obtained permission to borrow it for you."

"For me?" the girl asked.

"Yes," the dragon replied. "For, once you have found the Iron Rod, you must grab hold of it and not let go until the destruction is over."

"The destruction?" the girl said.

"The city will be destroyed. It has nothing to do with you, but you must not be there when it happens," the dragon said. "When it is over, throw the Iron Rod back into the sea."

"Throw the Iron Rod…" the girl said. "But it must be enormous! How could I even lift it?"

"The Iron Rod changes according to what is needed," the dragon said. "The Sea King's daughter even uses it as a needle sometimes. But that matters not. Do you understand all else I have said?"

The girl nodded.

"Do not forget," the dragon said. The forest fragrances of pine trees drifted around them. The dragon looked at her once more.

"I will always remember you," he said. Then he leaped into the air and flew away, the girl's tears blurring her last sight of him.

Many years passed, and, while she never forgot the dragon, his warning faded in significance. The girl grew to be a woman, married, had a child, and was quite happy. The woman was bestowed many honors and accolades throughout her life, but her daughter brought her greater joy than any of them. So, even though it was not tradition, after her husband died, the woman went to live with her newly married daughter in the city.

The woman, who was now old, did not enjoy city life. The city seemed coldhearted to her—merchants were ruthless in their dealings and masters callous to their servants, and all called her naive when she objected. However, she was content enough, and they lived in harmony together.

Then the old woman's daughter had a baby of her own. But, alas, she did not live through childbirth. So, as the old woman held the new baby tenderly, she rained tears of sorrow and joy upon it, and the baby's first bath was the unusual mixture of love and loss. For the birth of her beloved grandchild was just as the dragon had told her, the greatest joy and sadness at the same time.

And remembering this, the old woman began to watch the eyes of the stone lions of the city. She worried for others, warning any who would listen to her: "When the lions' eyes turn red," she told people, "the city will be destroyed." But no one believed her. As time went on, she became the laughingstock of the city. Embarrassed, her son-in-law pleaded and yelled by turns for her to stop her warnings, but the old woman did not.

Finally, an unkind man decided to taunt her with more than words. When she arrived at the statues, he took out a jar of red paint and began to splash it upon the eyes of the lions. "They're red now!" he mocked. "Should we be scared? Will the city be destroyed now?"

The old woman stood silently for a long moment, then she ran back to her home, grabbed her prepared bag of possessions, and begged her son-in-law to flee with her. Her son-in-law, who had heard what had happened, felt he had borne enough disgrace. He stormed out, telling her he regretted ever marrying her daughter and that she and the baby were not welcome in his house. So, tying the baby to her chest, the old woman left for the seashore.

The nearest island was nothing more than a giant rock with the barest scrub of green. As the old woman approached in a rowboat, the birds swooped away in a billowing black curve and she saw that in the middle of the empty rock grew a strange tree. It was straight and branchless, and when the old woman got nearer, she realized it was made of metal. It was the Iron Rod.

As soon as her fingers grazed the cold metal, the earth began to grumble. The old woman quickly wrapped one arm around the Iron Rod, clasping her grandchild protectively with the other.

And she was just in time. For, as if all the earth dragons were waking from nightmares, the grumbles became snarls and the sea began to bellow. Huge waves crested and covered them, leaving the old woman gasping. She clung even tighter to the Iron Rod and the baby, who only stared up at her grandmother with eyes as old as a mountain.

But the grandmother's eyes were fixed on the seashore. Even from the island, she could see the land rear toward the sky and the tall buildings collapse and crumble as if made of sand. Above the thunderous destruction, she could hear screams and shrieks, and when the old woman closed her eyes, the salt water on her face was not only from the ocean waves.

Finally, after what seemed like hours, the roars began to quiet and the old woman raised her head. The baby began to whimper, and slowly, the old woman loosened her hold on the Iron Rod.

As soon as she no longer touched the metal, the Iron Rod began to shrink. It grew smaller and smaller until it seemed nothing more than a blade of grass. The old woman reached down and saw the Iron Rod was now a needle, fine and delicate. Silently, she threw the needle into the sea. A wave surged upward to catch it, and as it did, another wave pushed the rowboat toward the island, making it drift straight to her.

The old woman returned to the city. But it could not

be called a city, for it was, as the dragon had predicted, destroyed. The few who had survived crawled out to cry at her feet. "Forgive us," they sobbed. "We should have listened to you." The old woman wept with them, finding no solace in having been right, for her son-in-law was among the dead.

After burying her son-in-law, the old woman left the city. People treated her as a prophet or a sage, and she knew she was neither. All she wished was to raise her granddaughter, so small and precious, away from harm and she remembered a mountain she had visited in her youth.

"There," the old woman said to the baby in her arms. "That is where I will keep you safe."

So they went to the mountain. And there, on the mountain whose top seemed to touch the moon, the old woman found peace and contentment. For her grandchild grew up protected and away from danger, and the only wish the old woman had was for that to never change.

"And did it?" the stonecutter asked, his keen eyes looking at Amah in sympathy.

"Stories cannot tell all," she said, and shrugged with heaviness, and the stonecutter saw her eyes suddenly haunted with worry.

"I disagree," the stonecutter said, his hand reaching to pat Amah's. "I think stories tell everything."

CHAPTER

20

How could this be happening to him? His breath could snap trees, his strength could hold up the earth! He was the Black Tortoise of Winter! The heavens and the sea honored him! He, the indestructible, the mighty!

But he felt the force on his back from the enormous—what was it? What was pinning him down, pressing on him with so much weight that he could not move? What could be so heavy that he, the great Black Tortoise, the strongest of all beasts, could not lift it?

His limbs struck outward, tearing into nothingness. He

craned his neck and snapped at the unseen object, his breath creating a crackling of ice on his shell.

He tried again to rise, but his arms and legs only sank into a slippery smoothness, like a deep silk pillow swallowing his limbs.

Who would dare do this to him? Who would dare insult him this way? Who would be this foolish, this arrogant, this devious, this...mad?

Not a beast. Not an immortal. Only a human.

Did this human not know that the Black Tortoise was forever? Oh, how he would make this human pay! For all eternity, the human would regret making the Black Tortoise of Winter so...so...

Helpless.

CHAPTER
21

BaiMa galloped through the gates of the City of Bright Moonlight. With Lady Meng as a companion, they had easily found shelter for the evening, and they had been riding most of the day. The wind and snow had howled around them, whipping the trees as well as their faces. So even BaiMa was eager when the city began to swell in the distance. The grand palace rose above the rest of the city like a mountain, the thick snow lying on its tiered roofs like heavy clouds. With a triumphant yell from Yishan, BaiMa had flown toward the city.

The stone lions that flanked either side of the gates

were wearing wigs and beards of snow, and they grinned as the horse passed through. The lions were the only ones with smiles, however, as all the other inhabitants of the city just stared at them with awe or horror—Pinmei was not sure which.

Almost wordlessly, people jumped out of their way, and Lady Meng did not even have to slow the horse. The common stone houses and the white snow were a gray blur, and BaiMa's hooves on the black brick road made a metallic noise, almost like the clinking of coins. Ahead, Pinmei saw a dull crimson barrier that stretched for miles. *That's the wall around the palace grounds*, Pinmei thought, remembering Amah's stories. *That's the Inner City and everything else is the Outer City. It's supposed to be like a city inside a city.*

"A walled city for the king of Bright Moonlight, the Vast Wall for the emperor," Yishan said in a mocking tone. "Rulers love walls, don't they?"

"*Halt!*" a voice, harsh and commanding, rang out above the sound of BaiMa's striking hooves.

Lady Meng pulled the horse to a stop, and Pinmei turned to see two guards on either side of the gate of the Inner City, neither of whom she had noticed before.

"I am here to see the king," Lady Meng said with the aristocratic dignity of an empress. From the corner of her eye, Pinmei saw Lady Meng nudge Yishan with her elbow, a warning for silence.

"The king is not seeing anyone," the guard said. Even though he was supposed to be the king's guard, his helmet had the emblem of the emperor—the face of a snarling tiger, the metal already turning green.

"He will see me," Lady Meng said. She pushed down the hood of her cloak and looked directly at him, letting the full force of her beauty and rank pour upon him like a waterfall. Indeed, the guard looked dazed and overwhelmed, and Pinmei suddenly realized how even a hero who would not be stopped by the fear of turning into ice could be slowed by a beautiful woman.

"Well, maybe—" the guard began to stammer.

"We aren't supposed to let anyone into the Inner City," the other guard cut in.

Lady Meng shifted her gaze, tossing her hair so it made a black cloud above them. Tiny jewels of snow sparkled around her.

"I am not 'anyone,'" she said with regal authority.

"No…yes…" the second guard said, equally bewildered by Lady Meng. "It's just the king—"

"Would be angered to hear that I was delayed in such a vulgar way," Lady Meng said, her voice the hypnotic sound of ocean waves. "Don't you think you'd better let me through?"

The guards looked at each other, confused.

Like a flying arrow, a small dark blur darted toward the guards. It was the swallow! It pecked at their helmets, twittering and flapping. Pinmei gave a small shriek of surprise, but the sound was lost as the guards yelped and clattered, waving their arms like crabs about to be dropped in a pot.

Lady Meng did not hesitate. With a quick command, BaiMa jumped through the gates and galloped into the Inner City.

CHAPTER
22

Yishan's laughter echoed across the empty courtyard. Pinmei craned her neck to see if the guards would follow them, but all she saw was a mist of snow. Perhaps the guards would think they were a dream.

When they passed a second courtyard, BaiMa slowed and Lady Meng looked up into the sky. Yishan and Pinmei followed her gaze until they finally saw what she was looking for. A small black dot circled above them.

"Thank you," Lady Meng said to the swallow. "Now the king, please."

The swallow led them to another empty courtyard,

then over an arched stone bridge of the same color as the frozen water beneath. BaiMa's steps made a hollow, mournful echo, and when the swallow stopped in front of a red carved door, they heard the unmistakable sound of weeping. Lady Meng hesitated, but pushed open the door.

They were in the throne room. Even though they were out of the wind, the room did not feel much warmer, and Pinmei was surprised by its starkness. The row of windows cast a cold white light, making everything within look like a shadow puppet. A tearful queen was being led out of the room by frozen-faced women, and the king sat stiffly on his throne, his eyes fixed on a paper clutched in his hands.

But the creaking of the door forced the king to look up, and when he saw the visitors, his face lit with surprised recognition, melting his stiffness.

"MengHai!" the king said, standing and reaching to pull Lady Meng up from her low bow. "What are you doing here?"

"KaiJae," Lady Meng said, grasping his arms in greeting. She glanced at the floating silk swirls of the departing women. "Why is the queen upset?"

"We just received some bad news. The emperor has conscripted the men of a village north of here and we"—the king hesitated and glanced around warily—"and we... have friends there."

Those must be some close friends, Pinmei thought. She felt she shouldn't be listening, but how else would they know when to ask about the dragon's pearl? She bit her lip and glanced over at Yishan. He, like her, had kneeled in a bowing position. He shrugged at her. They were unnoticed and forgotten, but this was not the time to interrupt.

"But it matters not," the king continued, shaking his head as if to clear it. His face took on an expression of alarm. "You must not be here. MengHai, you must leave right away!"

"Leave?" Lady Meng said. "I cannot leave until I know what happened to Wan. Tell me, how did he die?"

"He is dead?" the king gasped. "I thought the emperor took him to work on the Vast Wall..."

"The Vast Wall?" It was Lady Meng's turn to gasp. "Why was Wan working on the wall?"

"You did not get my message?" the king said.

Lady Meng shook her head. The king looked around again at the room, empty of all except them, and beckoned her closer. "Your husband was right about that meeting of kings. He said the Tiger King could not be trusted and insisted on going in my place," the king said in a fierce whisper. "The meeting was a trap. All the other kings were killed. The Tiger King made all his men the new kings, killed the old emperor, and then made himself the new emperor—the ruler of all."

"But what of Wan?" Lady Meng pressed.

"Wan was not killed," the king said. "For some reason, when he reached Wan, the Tiger King dropped his sword, grabbed your husband by the collar, and ripped his shirt. Then the Tiger King held a piece of the shirt in his hands, laughed, threw Wan to the ground, and told his men to take him away."

"Ripped his shirt," Lady Meng whispered, and Pinmei thought about the dragon shirt Lady Meng had sewn. It had failed to protect her husband.

"And then, not long after, he became invincible," the king said, scowling. "The Tiger King had always been a fierce warrior, but suddenly swords bounced off him and he could toss trees."

"And boys," Yishan added grimly to Pinmei. She grimaced. Was Amah with this emperor now, a man who didn't sound like a man at all? Pinmei swallowed and pressed her hand over Amah's bracelet as if she were hiding it.

"Now that he is emperor, the mountains bleed red where he has whipped them to make room for his Vast Wall," the king continued, either not hearing Yishan or ignoring him. "And men like your husband toil for him there night and day."

"Then I must go to the Vast Wall," Lady Meng said without hesitation. "I will find him, alive or dead."

"Wherever you go," the king said, "you and your friends must go immediately. It is not safe here, MengHai."

"But we just got here," Yishan said, lifting his head with indignation. Pinmei frowned in agreement. They still needed to ask about the dragon's pearl!

The king looked directly at them for the first time, and Pinmei's protests were temporarily forgotten in her surprise. The king's face was white and gaunt, and the deep shadows of his eyes looked as if they had been painted with smoke. He looked more like a ghost than a king.

"You don't understand," he said. "This is no place for children or friends. The emperor..."

The door to the throne room burst open, and with a biting gust of cold air, a servant flew to stand before the king.

"The emperor is here!" the servant girl gasped.

CHAPTER

23

"How close?" the king demanded.

"Just arrived at the gate," the servant girl said, breathing heavily. "Probably coming through the first courtyard now."

"Quickly, Yanna," the king said to the girl. "Take Lady Meng and these children to the Hall of Distant Clouds before the emperor or his men see them. They are friends and they must stay out of sight until after..."

Yanna, who did not seem much older than Pinmei, nodded with the shrewdness of an adult. Pinmei glanced back and forth between the King and Yanna, feeling like a mouse lost in the snow. But when the others rose in unison, she followed quickly, and the king led them to a door at the back of the room.

"Bring them through the Long Walkway; the emperor will take the other path," the king said to the girl. He turned to Lady Meng and the children. "Yanna will see that you are comfortable and well taken care of. I will send word when it is safe for you to leave. Go quickly."

"And Yanna," the king called as they turned to leave, "make sure you warn them about the western side of the walkway."

She nodded and pushed them through the doorway. They rushed through the halls of the palace, Lady Meng's robes flowing behind her like silken water, to another door. Then, to Pinmei's surprise, Yanna led them outside to a covered, meandering corridor. In warm weather, the richly decorated pathway was probably a delightful way to take a relaxed stroll through the garden. But now, with the biting wind and the endless landscape of white, the walkway's bends and length were more of an annoyance, and the fleeing group kept slipping on its curves.

Pinmei's thoughts twisted and turned like their running steps. The emperor was here? If the emperor was here... was Amah here too?

"What did the king mean when he said to warn us about the walkway?" Yishan said, huffing to keep up with Yanna's fast pace. "Something about the western side?"

Yanna slowed and looked behind them, the covered pathway stretching beyond them like a dragon's backbone.

"I think we're far enough away now," she said, stopping. "And you probably should know as soon as possible because it's important."

Lady Meng gave a grateful sigh, glad to rest, but Pinmei and Yishan looked at Yanna curiously.

"We are on the Long Walkway," Yanna said, speaking as if they were very young children. "This walkway divides the palace garden in half—in kind of a twisty way, of course—but still, in two."

"I think that's pretty obvious," Yishan said. Even though he was breathing heavily, his mocking tone was still clear. Pinmei nudged him.

"This is the eastern side," Yanna said, ignoring Yishan and motioning toward the left. She waved to her right. "That is the western side."

Pinmei looked back and forth at both sides of the walkway. There did not seem to be a big difference between the two sides.

"So?" Yishan said.

"While the emperor is here, you are never to go on the western side of the Long Walkway," Yanna said, raising her voice for emphasis. "You must never, ever cross the walkway to the western side."

"Why?" Yishan asked. "What happens if we do?"

"If you do, you're dead!" Yanna snorted. "The emperor declared he'd kill anyone and their family if they were found on the western side while he's here. So don't cross the walkway. Do you understand?"

Pinmei looked again at the western side of the walkway. It was blanketed with thick snow, iced over, and glittering like a diamond, but she still did not see anything unusual about it.

"No, I don't understand," Lady Meng said, her lovely face frowning in confusion. "The western side, the eastern side? Why is it important?"

"It's important to the emperor," Yanna said, turning to lead them farther. "And, while he's here, that's all that matters."

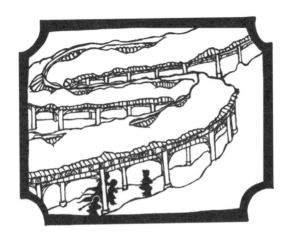

CHAPTER
24

Ignoring Yishan's further questions, Yanna hurried them onward, though not as quickly as before. However, Pinmei's thoughts continued to race. Eastern side, western side? Why? Did it have anything to do with Amah? If Amah was here, could they find her? Pinmei gazed upward, trying to calm herself.

It was then that she noticed the beams and ceiling of the corridor were painted with hundreds of scenes from different stories. The Old Man of the Moon with his bag of red threads, the Spirit of the Mountain holding up the moon as only he could…Pinmei recognized them all. Yanna noticed her gaze.

"The Long Walkway is supposed to show a picture from every important legend," she said. "They say a new painting appears right before a story of greatness is about to be told."

"I wonder what kind of magic can do that," Lady Meng said, looking up in appreciation.

"I don't know if I believe it," the servant girl said, even while urging them forward, "but these were all created over a hundred years ago by the master painter Chen, who was supposed to have a magic paintbrush or ink-stone or something like that. He even painted a picture of a dragon that came to life."

"Is that in one of the paintings?" Yishan said, teasing.

"Yes," Pinmei said softly. She had seen the image of a red dragon flying off a paper as they had rushed pass.

"Anyway," Yanna said, not hearing Pinmei's whisper, "it's not like anyone would be able to prove it either way. You'd have to know thousands and thousands of stories to know all the pictures. I walk here all the time and I don't know any of the ones we just passed."

"None?" Pinmei said, her shock making her voice louder than she'd intended.

Yishan gave a sly grin. "I bet Pinmei knows all of them," he said.

Yanna turned to look at Pinmei, who would have flushed if her cheeks had not already been red from the cold. "Do you?" Yanna asked.

Pinmei gave a tiny shrug and nodded.

Yanna stopped walking. "We can take another rest," she said, and then waved up toward one of the ceiling beams. She looked at Pinmei. "Do you know that one?"

It had begun to snow again, and despite the walkway's canopy, the snowflakes flew in like fine silver threads. But Pinmei could still easily see the painting. It was a picture of a young girl and her parents standing before a king. In the girl's arms, there was a large bowl with a smiling fish in it.

"It's the Story of How a Girl Brought Joy to the Heart of a King," Pinmei said.

"Well, now you have to tell it," Yanna said, and a crooked smile formed on her face. It fit her face so perfectly that Pinmei realized Yanna's serious manner was a new occurrence. "Can you?"

"Of course she can," Yishan said, and Lady Meng nodded in agreement. Pinmei hesitated, but looked at their expectant faces—proud, encouraging, daring—and felt the stone of Amah's bracelet on her wrist, strong and smooth. Pinmei took a deep breath, and when she exhaled, the air steamed from her mouth, curving like the tail of a dragon before disappearing. She began the story.

THE STORY OF HOW A GIRL BROUGHT JOY TO THE HEART OF A KING

When the first king of the City of Bright Moonlight came to power, the people had no love for their new ruler. The past ruler had taxed them heavily and punished them harshly, and they had no hope for better. So when word came that the new king was coming to visit, all trembled.

"He's coming to see if he can raise our taxes!" a woman wailed.

"Anything he sees, he will take for a tribute," another cried.

The villagers began to panic and hid their most valued possessions. Gold ingots, ivory chopsticks, even prized crickets were secreted away. Anything beloved or cherished was put out of sight.

One girl in the village had a special treasure. It was a fish. But it was not an ordinary fish. It was a fish of great beauty, silver like the moon and as lively as a butterfly in spring. The girl claimed she had found the fish in a rubbish pile outside a rich home when she traveled to a far town, but no one believed her. Even when she pointed at the fine scar that ran through the fish's fin where she said she had mended it, her parents told her to stop being ridiculous.

Nevertheless, the fish was admired and beloved by the whole village. The youngest child to the oldest, grumpiest elder would come daily just to see it. "Your little fish," the girl's mother told her, shaking her head with a smile. "It just brings joy to the heart."

So, of course, when the news of the king's visit was heard, all expected the girl to hide the fish. "I can help you make a special cover to hide the tub," one villager offered. "There might be room in my hollow tree if you want to hide it there," another said. But the girl shook her head. Instead, she kneeled beside her fish, deep in thought.

"You must hurry," her mother scolded her. "If you don't find a place to hide your fish, the king will take it when he comes."

"He may have it," the girl said. "It will be my gift."

"What?" her father said. "Don't be silly. The king doesn't need your fish. He will just take it and your treasure will be lost."

"How can you say that?" the girl said. "A king needs joy brought to his heart too."

The parents looked at each other, and nothing more about the fish was said.

When the king arrived, he was saddened by his reception. He knew the people did not trust him, but he did not know how to gain their faith. He received each obligatory gift knowing that the good wishes that went with it were false and the respectful bows were shallow. *It is not even worth trying*, the king thought, gloom overwhelming him. *I will return to the palace today.*

"More villagers, Your Majesty," a servant said.

The king looked up, expecting to see another family with smiles of clenched teeth. Instead, he saw a glistening fish frolicking in the water. It jumped a perfect arch, its scales shimmering a rainbow, then dived straight down—splashing the king with such glee he could not help laughing aloud.

"See?" the girl said to her parents. "I told you."

The king wiped the drops of water from his face, but the smile remained. "What do you mean?" the king said before the girl's parents could hush her. "What did you tell them?"

Slowly, and uncomfortably for the parents, the story was told. The king wiped his face again, but this time the wetness was not from the splashes of the fish.

"You are right," the king told the girl, and his deep black eyes met her shining ones. "A king does need joy brought to his heart. I thank you for doing so."

"But I cannot take your beloved fish from you," he continued. "You may keep it."

"Oh no," the girl said, and the parents put in hastily, "it's our tribute gift."

"It would be unfair to the other villagers," the king's assistant murmured, "and it would break tradition."

"Ah…yes," the king said. He looked again at the twinkling fish. "Then let me make it a gift. I will set it free in the lake, and it can continue to bring joy to the hearts of all the villagers."

"But what of your own?" the girl asked.

"The fish has already brought joy to my heart," the king said, "as have you."

And all the villagers who witnessed this exchange felt a stirring within them as well. Perhaps, they thought, they had judged this new king too quickly. They began to whisper kinder and more hopeful words about the king, and those words traveled with him as he carried on his tour. Because instead of returning to the palace, the king continued going to each village so he could become the leader he wished to be, heartened by the joy brought by the fish.

"I like that," Lady Meng said as Pinmei finished. "Especially because the first king of the City of Bright Moonlight is known for being the greatest ruler in the city's history. All his descendants, including King KaeJae, revere him."

"Well, it's too bad it's just a story," Yanna said, her crooked smile appearing again. The wind loosened a lock of her hair, and it danced freely among the flying snowflakes. "But it was good one."

CHAPTER
25

The Long Walkway ended in a courtyard flanked by red-columned buildings, their dignity belied by the distinctive noise of snoring. Yanna marched forward and pushed open the carved doors of the main structure. Inside, a lone servant blinked up at them.

"Fishing in empty water, are you?" Yanna scolded. "How dare you sleep when you should be working!"

The servant, a graying woman, threw herself on the floor keening with apologies.

Yanna shook her head and sighed. "These are the king's guests," she said with a tone of authority. "They'll be staying for at least a couple of days. Start the coal heaters, and make sure their rooms are comfortable."

The servant nodded and bowed. As Yanna waved her hand in dismissal, the servant snatched up her fallen broom and scurried away.

"I probably saved her life," Yanna said with a hint of her crooked smile. "This place has been empty for months. You could freeze to death sleeping here."

But Pinmei only looked at Yanna curiously. She was scarcely half a head taller than Yishan, but she ordered servants about as if she had been at the palace for decades.

As if hearing her thoughts, Lady Meng spoke.

"Have you been here a long time?" she asked Yanna. "It's unusual for someone so young to have so much responsibility."

Yanna's impish grin returned. "That's your nice way of saying I'm not old enough to be the head of the king's servants," she said. "I'm not. I worked in the kitchen, at first."

"From the kitchen to the king's attendant?" Yishan said. "That's quite a jump! Why were you working in the kitchen?"

"My father got into some trouble—a long time ago—before the Tiger King became emperor." Yanna was starting to stammer, but she took a deep breath and continued. "I was just happy to find a place where I could stay."

"Where did you come from?" Lady Meng asked kindly.

"Oh," Yanna said vaguely, "just a village by the sea."

"The sea is far away," Lady Meng said. "You traveled quite a distance."

"I rode a horse," Yanna said, and her eyes softened with the memory.

"It must be quite a horse," Yishan said, watching Yanna's face closely. It had taken on a wistful, dreamy expression.

"Oh, it was," Yanna said. "The most beautiful white... But it's gone now. It was never mine anyway... though it didn't belong to the king either..."

A beautiful white horse? Pinmei thought. *That sounds like BaiMa! Could he have...* But Lady Meng was talking.

"The king took your horse?" Lady Meng said, slightly shocked. "I can't believe KaeJae..."

"No, no!" Yanna said, shaking her head rapidly. "I meant the Tiger Emperor, not the king of Bright Moonlight. It was the Tiger Emperor when he was king who wanted the horse but..." She looked at their confused faces and quickly continued. "Anyway, when I got here, I was able to get a job in the palace kitchen, just scrubbing floors, washing dishes—that sort of thing."

"So how did you get to be the king's attendant?" Yishan asked.

"I volunteered. The Tiger Emperor took all the men to work on the wall," Yanna said, "so that left only old women and girls here at the palace."

"There are some guards," Yishan protested.

"The king can't trust them," Yanna snorted. "They're all spies for the emperor!"

"The emperor is spying on the king? Why?" Yishan said. "He could just kill the king, like he did all the others."

"No, he can't, because he needs him," Yanna said.

"Why?" they all, even Pinmei, asked in unison.

"The king said you were friends," she said, and Pinmei was surprised to see Yanna looking directly at her. "I think I can trust you."

Yishan said, "Of course," but it was only when Pinmei nodded that Yanna continued.

"Well," Yanna said, dropping her voice to a whisper and looking around hastily. "Remember what I said about the western side of the walkway?" She waited until they all nodded at her. "When the emperor comes, he and the king go out to the western side of the garden—and all his guards have to camp on the eastern side of the Long Walkway."

"Even his guards don't go to the western side?" Yishan asked.

Yanna shook her head. "No one crosses over to the western side when the emperor is here," she said. "Not a servant or a guard—they wouldn't even dare shoot an arrow. Like I said, you'd be killed if you did. I bet even a bird would be killed if it were there at the same time as the emperor."

"Does the emperor come often?" Lady Meng asked.

Yanna nodded. "But only for one night, when the moon is full," she said. "He leaves right after, as fast as he can."

"And the emperor is here now?" Yishan said, disbelief creeping into his voice.

"Well, it's a full moon tonight," Yanna said, shrugging. "That's when he and the king go out to the garden, alone, at night, when the moon rises."

"But why?" Lady Meng said. "What do he and the king do?"

Yanna shrugged and began leading them through the empty hall to a chamber door. "I asked the king once, and he told me it was safer if I didn't know," she said. "But whatever it is, only the king can do it and the emperor needs him. That's why no one is allowed to harm the king, but the king isn't allowed to do anything either."

"What do you mean?" Lady Meng asked.

"Well, the palace might as well be a prison," Yanna said. "The king can't leave, and no one is ever allowed to see him."

"We did," Yishan said.

"That's true," Yanna said, frowning. She stopped at the door and opened it. "I hope you don't get in trouble for it."

CHAPTER
26

Pinmei and Yishan had been treated to a dinner of new enjoyments. In a lacquered box brought by the gray-haired and grim servant, there had been tea-stained eggs, pickled plums, and cold slices of aromatic roast chicken that made Pinmei afraid she would embarrass herself by drooling over it all. But even while they ate, Pinmei's thoughts nibbled at her. How could they find out if Amah was here? As the servant refilled their cups with golden tea, Pinmei longed to speak to Yishan alone. So when Lady Meng soon retired to her bed, taking the servant with her, Pinmei looked at Yishan eagerly.

"Yishan," Pinmei said, "if the emperor is here, I think..."

"Amah?" Yishan said, nodding. "I was thinking the same thing."

"She might be here!" Pinmei said, her words bubbling like heated porridge. "The emperor could have come here from our mountain..."

"Stopping at a couple of villages to collect men on the way," Yishan said, agreeing. "But there's a good chance he just came here with a small troop of soldiers and sent the rest of them, with Amah, off to...wherever."

The wind gave a piercing scream, and both Pinmei and Yishan were silent. Was Amah in a dungeon, in the dark and alone? Or out in the freezing snow, shivering? Pinmei placed her hand over the cold jade bracelet on her wrist, her fingers curling around it.

"Yanna said the soldiers camp out on the eastern side of the Long Walkway," Pinmei said. "So if we just follow the walkway, we could find the camp easily."

"But to find Amah, we'd have to sneak among the soldiers," Yishan said. "And Yanna also said the emperor is out there too."

Pinmei looked out the window. The branches on the trees were being flung about by the wind, swaying toward her like bony fingers clawing at a small animal. She shivered, pulling the bracelet on and off her wrist.

"The emperor and his men are only here for one night," she said. "That means we only have tonight to look for Amah."

Yishan rubbed his chin. "So when everyone is sleeping," he said, "we'll have to creep out of here to the soldiers' camp and sneak around to look for Amah."

Pinmei nodded. Her hands cupped Amah's bracelet like a nest and the stone began to warm.

"We'll have to be very careful," Yishan warned, "and very, very quiet."

Pinmei turned to look at Yishan, putting the bracelet on her arm. Then she tossed her braid, which had always reminded her of a long mouse tail.

"I can do that," Pinmei said.

Yishan looked back at her and grinned.

CHAPTER
27

"Ah, they feed me much better since you arrived," the stonecutter said as the dungeon door slammed closed. He picked up a bowl of rice and pushed it toward Amah.

"A small bowl of rice every other day," Amah said, taking the bowl, "does not seem like good feeding to me."

"They used to forget for three, four days—sometimes a week," the stonecutter said. "And now, they leave a light. It is because of you, of course."

"Me?" Amah said, scooping the rice with her cold fingers.

"Yes," the stonecutter said. "You misjudge those who

honor you. They do not think you can predict the future or save them from catastrophe. They honor you because you are the Storyteller."

"It does not seem like something that would earn the respect of men such as these," Amah said.

"Almost all men respect the Storyteller," the stonecutter said. "You can make time disappear. You can bring us to places we have never dreamed of. You can make us feel sorrow and joy and peace. You have great magic."

"You flatter me," Amah said. "I do not think I am what you say."

The stonecutter laughed. "How can you not be?" he said. "Don't the soldiers treat you as kindly as they can? Are you not covered by a guard's own coat right now?"

"How selfish I am," Amah said. "You have been cold much longer than me. You should have this coat."

"The guard gave it to you, Storyteller," the stonecutter said. "Keep it. Instead, give me another story."

"Very well," Amah said. "What kind of story would you like?"

"Tell me a story about eating something delicious," the stonecutter said, "so I can imagine I am eating something other than plain rice."

THE STORY OF THE
STOLEN BITE OF PEACH

Emperor Zu was called the Son of the Heavens because he was indeed somehow related to the immortal Queen Mother of the Heavens. And even though the relation must have been distant, the Queen Mother still looked upon him with great favor. For his sixtieth birthday celebration, the Queen Mother came. A full chariot pulled by unicorns burst from a cloud and descended. The thousands of acrobats, singers, dancers, and guests froze at a shocked standstill. However, while the light of the stars on the Queen Mother's crown was brighter than all the lanterns combined, it was the peach she held in her hands that everyone stared at.

"Zu," the Queen Mother said, "your character is too flawed for me to grant you immortality, so instead I bring you this peach of longevity. This peach will grant you nine hundred and ninety-nine more years of life. I hope with these extra years, you will be able to merit immortality."

All, including the emperor, sank to the floor in defer-
ence, and one of the queen's companions had to nudge
a servant to rise in order to take the peach. As the
emperor stammered his gratitude, the Queen Mother
nodded to him and gave the sea of bowed heads a glance
of acknowledgment. Then the unicorns reared and
leaped and she and her entourage disappeared back
into the sky.

For a moment, the emperor and his guests could
only stare up at the heavens. If it were not for the
peach, all would have doubted the reality of the Queen
Mother's visit. But the glorious golden peach was casting a warm glow. The emperor, already licking his lips,
waved his hand for the peach to be brought to him.

The crowd parted and watched in hushed silence as
the trembling servant carried the peach as if leading
a procession. The sweet fragrance wafted through the
air like an intoxicating wine, and it was not only the
emperor's mouth that watered.

But just as the peach was almost within arm's distance of the emperor, someone broke through the
mesmerized crowd and grabbed it! After a brief
stunned moment, the emperor barked an order, and
the guards clamored.

They swarmed upon the attempted thief, who collapsed to the floor. But with him fell the peach. It rolled on the floor toward the emperor, and all gazed in horror as they saw that a bite had been taken out of it!

For while the moment of shock had been short, it had been long enough. The golden skin of the peach had been torn open, and where a chunk of flesh was now missing, a sweet, sticky juice was dripping like crystal beads gliding off a string. The emperor would not take the first bite of his peach.

Enraged, the emperor had the thief brought before him. To everyone's surprise, it was a magistrate who was distantly connected to the emperor by marriage. By all accounts, he was well liked. But all favor had disappeared with the bite of the peach.

"How dare you take a bite of my peach!" the emperor roared. "I shall have you executed!"

"Forgiveness, Your Exalted Majesty," the magistrate said, prostrating himself. "But if I have eaten from the peach of longevity, how can I be killed?"

"Fool!" the emperor said. "You have stolen some extra years of life, but you are not invincible! That bite of peach may protect you from sickness and age, but you can still be killed."

"Ah," said the magistrate, who, contrary to the emperor's words, was not a fool. "But that peach was given to you by the Queen Mother to give you time to become worthy of immortality. Do you think she would be pleased if the first thing you do upon receiving it is to order me to my death?"

At that, the emperor hesitated, for there was truth in his words. He grunted with annoyance. It occurred to him that he had yet to eat his peach and that he should consume it before any more disasters occurred.

"Just take him away," the emperor thundered. "And bring me my peach!"

And so the official was taken away and the emperor finally received his peach. And while the emperor ate it with much delight, even he must have wondered how much sweeter the peach would have been if he had gotten the first bite.

"But Emperor Zu did not live an extra nine hundred and ninety-nine years," the stonecutter said. "He was the last of the Min emperors, killed by the soldiers of Emperor Shang."

"Well, that just proves Emperor Zu was right," Amah

said. "The peach could keep him from getting old or sick, but he could still be killed. Even immortality is not invincibility."

"That's true," the stonecutter said. "I wonder what happened to that official. Executed later, do you think?"

"I don't know," Amah said slowly. "I wonder."

"I wonder how many extra years that official stole with that one bite," the stonecutter said, laughing as he brought the rice bowl to his face. "Perhaps he is alive still and wishes he had taken another bite!"

"Perhaps," Amah said, but she did not laugh as she swallowed her rice.

CHAPTER
28

Yishan and Pinmei stepped onto the Long Walkway. In the distance, there was the glow of many campfires. Without a word, Yishan pointed to them. Pinmei nodded in agreement. Just as she had thought, the soldiers would be easy to find.

The screaming wind had quieted to moans, but it did not calm Pinmei. Instead, she felt as if the sky were in a fitful slumber and about to awaken in a rage.

They scurried down the corridor in silence, the sound of their feet hidden by the lamenting wind. Pinmei found herself looking from side to side. Western side. Eastern side. *No one crosses over to the western side*, Yanna had said. *You'd be killed if you did.* Pinmei veered toward the eastern side as much as possible.

As soon as the silhouettes of tents came into view, they left the covered pathway to make a wide circle around the camp. As they crept closer, Yishan shook his head at Pinmei, and she drooped with sudden heaviness. There were only a dozen or so tents, nowhere near large enough for an emperor's army. It was just a small troop, as Yishan had guessed. *Still, we have to check,* Pinmei thought.

The glow of the fires and the moonlight reflected on the snow made it almost as bright as morning, and they ran behind one of the tents to stay hidden. They could hear the rumbling snores of soldiers inside, like the growls of waiting beasts.

"Her tent would be guarded," Yishan whispered in her ear.

Pinmei nodded, and they both began to run, going from tent to tent, deeper and deeper into the camp. As they stopped to rest at another tent, Yishan nudged her and nodded toward a tent surrounded by the others. It was larger than the other tents and an imperial flag flew from the cask in front of it. But it was the two guards whom the children's eyes were fixed upon.

"Do you think Amah's in there?" Pinmei whispered.

"All we can do is check," he whispered back. "We'll run to the back of the tent, I'll sneak in, and you stand guard."

"How are you going to get in?" Pinmei whispered. Even from a distance, she could see the tent was anchored closely to the snow-cleared ground, the cloth tightly stretched without a wrinkle.

Yishan put his hand in his bag, which Pinmei had thought he was carrying, like she was, out of habit, and pulled out a small knife. He grinned at her. "Picked it up at your hut," he said. "Forgot to tell you."

Pinmei rolled her eyes at him. Then, after glancing around, they ran.

Pinmei held her breath the whole way. Was Amah in the tent? Could they reach her? Would someone catch them?

But they arrived in the shadow of the tent, and no one seemed to have noticed them. Yishan took out the knife again, and it glinted as it caught the light of a nearby campfire. Pinmei peered over his shoulder as he placed the tip of the knife against the taut tent.

But then, from nowhere, someone reached out and grabbed his hand!

CHAPTER
29

"Shhh!" a voice whispered in Pinmei's ear.

Pinmei swallowed her yelp of surprise and whipped her head around to look into familiar eyes. *Yanna!*

"What are you doing here?" Yishan whispered fiercely. Pinmei could only stare. Yanna looked nothing like she had earlier. She was no longer wearing her servants' dress; instead, her clothes were all black. Her hair was hidden on top of her head with a tightly knotted cloth.

"Me?" Yanna whispered back with incredulous amusement. "What about you two? Why are you trying to sneak into the commander's tent?"

"Commander's tent?" Pinmei said. She looked at the tent, and the ice butterflies in her stomach froze together into a crushing boulder. "We thought the tent was... We're looking for... prisoner... the emperor we thought maybe..."

Yanna's smile disappeared. "I was looking for prisoners too," she said, her face sad. "They aren't here. The emperor has sent them off to the Vast Wall already."

"Who are you looking for?" Yishan asked. "Your father?"

"No." Yanna shook her head. "I'm here for the king. I'm looking for his son."

"His son?" both Pinmei and Yishan said in unison, and Yanna quickly hushed them.

"The king sent him into hiding in a village north of here," Yanna said. "It was that village where the emperor collected his latest workers."

Which was why the queen was crying when we came, Pinmei realized. His son and the people who hid him must be the "close friends" the king had meant when he had spoken with Lady Meng. Suddenly, she understood the king's ashen face and stricken eyes.

"Did he send you to look?" Yishan said in an offended tone. "That's pretty rotten of him!"

"It was my idea," Yanna said, drawing herself up taller.

"And if it wasn't for you, I probably would never have offered."

"Me?" Yishan said.

"Not you," Yanna said, smirking at Yishan. She nodded over at Pinmei. "You!"

"Me?" Pinmei said, just as surprised.

"It was that story you told," Yanna said. "I started thinking about, and it made me feel ashamed. I've been working for the king all this time hoping that someday he could help my father, but I never thought about what I could do to help him. That story made me realize the king might be as worried about his son as I am about my father."

"So you volunteered to run in the middle of the night into a soldiers' camp?" Yishan shook his head.

"At least I am disguised," Yanna shot back. "I could see your hat with my eyes closed! Besides, if it weren't for me, you'd be crawling on top of the commander right now!"

"Shhh!" Pinmei warned.

Too late! A sword blade stabbed through the tent fabric and the *RIIIIPP* tore apart the quiet that had blanketed the entire camp.

"*Who's there?*" shouted the commander.

CHAPTER
30

"This way!" Yanna said, pulling them behind a rock sculpture. The camp was now alive and swarming, throngs of men starting to swell together like boils of a plague.

"I'll go first," Yanna said. "I'll lead them toward the main palace. Then you two go the other way. You'd best get your lady friend and leave right away. Get out of the City of Bright Moonlight as fast as you can. It won't take long for the emperor to find out you're here now."

"You're going to lead them away?" Pinmei gasped. "Yanna! You can't!"

"Don't worry about me," Yanna said. "Once they find out there were strangers here, they won't suspect me at all. I just have to get someplace to change clothes."

"B-but..." Pinmei stuttered. She looked at Yishan, who was strangely quiet. "But..."

"Just remember, no one crosses to the western side of the walkway," Yanna instructed. "No matter what you do, stay on this side. Do not cross the walkway!"

A bellow from the camp howled toward them and they looked at one another.

"Take care of yourselves out there," Yanna said, her crooked smile returning. Her eyes met Pinmei's, and suddenly, Pinmei found they were friends. "Make sure you put me in a story someday."

And she was off.

Pinmei watched as Yanna hollered and the soldiers began to chase her, a single running figure in the night, like a rabbit being chased by wolves.

"She'll be okay," Yishan said. "We're the ones in trouble. Yanna's right. We'd better get out of here."

He took off his hat and shoved it into his bag. Pinmei took a deep breath, and together they began to run.

The snow of the uncleared ground padded their footsteps, but nothing could muffle the pounding inside

Pinmei. They passed a tent. Then another. Pinmei could see the covered path of the Long Walkway.

Behind them yelled a voice.

"Over there!" the voice shouted, cutting into the night air as well as Pinmei's chest. "That way!"

Stomping and shouts clattered closer behind them. They were steps from the Long Walkway, but how would they ever make it all the way back? Pinmei's feet slipped and stumbled as she tried to run even more quickly. *Faster*, she told herself. *Faster.*

But the thunder behind them only grew louder, like an inescapable storm. Yishan turned his head to look at Pinmei, but his eyes widened at what he saw instead.

The soldiers were right there! They were like a pack of mad dogs, their torches flickering like demonic eyes and their swords glittering like sharp teeth.

"Children!" one of the soldiers spat with disgust. "Come here, you brats!"

He leaped and his hand clawed the cold wind between them. Annoyed, he snarled and the group of men behind him echoed his growls like hungry beasts. He lunged again, grabbing the sleeve of Pinmei's coat. She pulled with all her strength, but he only laughed.

"You're not getting away!" the soldier said in a tone

that would have been mocking if it weren't so vicious. He began to drag her to him. Pinmei screamed.

Then she felt Yishan pull her. He jerked her from the soldier with such force it threw her to the ground. When she looked up, breathless, Yishan was standing like a mountain between her and the crowd of soldiers.

"Yishan!" she screeched as she scrambled up. She pulled at Yishan, tugging him with all her might to lead him away. "Come on!"

He let himself be pulled a few steps, but he moved with such reluctance that she finally lifted her head to see what he was looking at. Then she too stopped.

The soldiers weren't following them! They stood all in a row alongside the Long Walkway, the fires from their torches trembling. What were they waiting for? Why were they just standing there?

Then Pinmei realized she was looking at the soldiers through the posts of the covered pathway. That meant she and Yishan were on the other side, the western side! She and Yishan had crossed the Long Walkway!

CHAPTER
31

"We're on the wrong side!" Pinmei whispered to Yishan.

They glanced at the soldiers, who were eerily quiet. Behind, another row of men formed. But none dared to cross the walkway. Instead, the soldiers simply stood flanking the corridor, all silently staring at them.

"We shouldn't be here!" Pinmei said, her voice still an urgent whisper. She began to tremble. "Yanna said not to cross the walkway."

"Too late," Yishan said grimly. He looked at her and she saw that he too was disturbed. "What should we do?"

The bleak faces of the soldiers watching them frightened her even more than being chased. Their eyes were fixed on them as if she and Yishan were ghosts.

"Let's go somewhere so we don't have to see them looking at us at least," she said.

Yishan nodded. They turned and walked into the garden, choosing a tree-covered footpath that would hide them from view. Round lanterns lit the zigzagging walkway, their glowing circles echoing the full moon above. The constellations glittered in the black sky, a star streaking across it like a shimmering loose thread.

"Beacon Fire," Yishan whispered, watching the shooting star with surprising intensity.

"What?" Pinmei asked. "What beacon?"

"Oh, it's just a constellation I suddenly remembered," Yishan said, and Pinmei saw his self-assurance had returned. In fact, he looked strangely confident. He looked around at the garden. "This place is big."

Pinmei nodded, but she was still shaking. They walked on. The branches above created a canopy patched with dark swatches of the sky, embroidered with the stars and falling snow. What were they going to do? Would they get out of here? How could they save Amah now?

Across the frozen lake, a pavilion was brightly lit. Pinmei

stared. Even from their distance she could see two silhou-ettes inside it. She gripped Yishan's arm.

"The emperor and the king!" Pinmei hissed.

Yishan squinted. "Looks like they're just talking," he said. "I wonder what they're talking about."

Pinmei continued to stare, the small figures like two stitches of embroidery thread on a vast tapestry. Could they be talking about Amah? Or the Luminous Stone? And the king—they never got to ask the king about the dragon's pearl. Maybe...

"Should we try to find out?" she squeaked. Was she crazy? But this might be their only chance! She placed her hand on her chest, letting her heart beat against the stone of Amah's bracelet.

"Good idea," Yishan said, nodding. "We're going to be killed for being on the wrong side of the walkway, so we might as well make it worth it."

Pinmei gulped. Still, she stepped forward and led Yishan onto the path with the silent and skilled stealth of a mouse.

CHAPTER
32

He was tired.

He had slashed and snapped, struck and roared, but it had done nothing. He had only beaten the air that slipped and slithered around him like smooth silk. Even his screams and howls seemed to have been smothered in that brilliant blankness.

His throat was raw from screaming. His arms and legs lay limp.

He was the Black Tortoise of Winter, indestructible and invincible.

But that did not matter.

His strength and power could not help him. There was nothing for him to fight, no one for him to conquer.

He could do nothing. Except...

He could do what he had never done before. He could do what he had never imagined he would ever have need for.

The gold glimmered at him, mocking and taunting. He closed his eyes.

Perhaps it was time for him to ask for help.

CHAPTER

33

"Do you think we could hide behind that?" Pinmei whispered right into Yishan's ear as she pointed to a large stone sculpture at the foot of the pavilion.

The sculpture, dark in the shadows, would hide them well, and it would place them close enough to hear everything, but it meant that they would have to run across the open pathway to get there. Yishan shrugged and gave her a doubtful motion with his hand. *I don't know*, he said to her with his eyes. *You decide.*

They could both see the emperor and the king clearly now, both of them in the well-lit pavilion as if they were standing on a stage. The king was motioning toward a carved chest, and both turned as he began to open it.

"*Now!*" she hissed into his ear, and gave him a push.

They dashed to the stone sculpture and crouched in its shadow. Had they been noticed?

They heard a growl of laughter. Pinmei quaked and fought to stifle a shriek.

"Good try, King KaiJae!" the emperor's voice said.

"The dragon's pearl is not the Luminous Stone you seek?" the king replied, and despite his formal tone, Pinmei could hear the devastation in his voice.

"A Luminous Stone could be a dragon's pearl," the emperor laughed again. "But this dragon's pearl is not a Luminous Stone."

Pinmei and Yishan looked at each other in dismay. The dragon's pearl wasn't the Luminous Stone? Then what was?

"I do not understand," the king said.

"Ha! Maybe if you took a swim at the Crystal Palace at Sea Bottom you could figure it out," the emperor chortled. "But I doubt it. You are not as smart as you think!"

"I am a fool when compared with Your Exalted Majesty," the king said in a dull, almost practiced tone.

"Liar!" the emperor said. "Admit it, you think yourself very clever because only you can read the Paper of Answers."

Paper of Answers! Pinmei sat up and almost gasped aloud. Did the king have the Paper of Answers? How could he? And what had the emperor meant about the Crystal Palace?

"I am not the only one who can read it," the king said.

"Yes, yes," the emperor said, and Pinmei could hear him waving his hand as if trying to swat a wasp, "I know! Immortals, or those with great fortune or peace or whatnot, can read it too, so you tell me. But because I cannot read it, you no doubt think you are much wiser than me."

"I would never..." the king began.

"But you are not!" the emperor continued, ignoring the king's protests. "Answer me, have not all my questions to the Paper confused you?"

"Tortoises, mountains holding moons, and needles under the sea? I would not even pretend to understand what you are asking," the king replied. "Except, of course, for your last question."

"Bah! Last time was a wasted question," the emperor said with a snort of irritation. "The Paper obviously didn't know the answer!"

"The Paper always knows," the king said immediately.

"Stories!" the emperor said, dismissing the king's words. "Only that word, repeated over and over again!

How could that be the secret to immortality? I even took the Storyteller too! But for nothing! Just a waste!"

Stories? Pinmei felt her thoughts swoop as if caught on the tail of a kite. The Paper had told the emperor that the secret to immortality was stories and that was why he had taken Amah! But Amah didn't know the secret of immortality! Did she?

"However, that was last time," the emperor said. "The Paper can attempt to redeem itself tonight."

"Yes, Your Exalted Majesty," the king said. They heard a rustling and the king stumble.

"Careful, you fool!" the emperor barked. "Keep that accursed Paper away from me."

"Yes, Your Exalted Majesty," said the king. "What is your question this time?"

"Ask the Paper," the emperor said, "if I will achieve immortality."

Pinmei heard the king shift, and both she and Yishan craned their necks to see him lean out of the pavilion, holding the Paper over the frozen lake.

"Will the emperor achieve immortality?" the king said in a loud voice. The full moon made a halo around his head, and only the soft reflected glow from the ice kept his face from being lost in shadow.

"What does it say?" the emperor demanded. "What does that line say?"

Pinmei watched the king gasp. The steam from his breath formed a silver-gray cloud that froze in the air. His eyes widened and his white hands tightened around the Paper.

"It says..." the king said in a strained tone. "It says yes."

CHAPTER

34

Pinmei and Yishan stared at each other, their horrified faces mirroring. The emperor would be immortal? Pinmei felt as if a snake had laid an egg in her stomach.

"How?" the emperor said, the excitement palpable in his voice. "When? Ask it when!"

"Your Exalted Majesty, you know the Paper answers only once," the king said.

"Yes, yes," the emperor said impatiently. "Only one question and only in the light of the full moon. Infernal thing!"

The wind, which had been silent, gave a weak whimper, as if too tired to even protest.

"Very well. I will wait," the emperor said, and in a more satisfied tone: "What is another moon when I will have eternity anyway?"

The king did not reply. Pinmei twisted again to see him gazing bleakly at the shadows on the icy lake, looking, she thought, as if he were seeing his own life of endlessly serving the emperor. The snow fell softly—tiny stars yielding their grasp on the sky.

"Meanwhile, I must make plans..." the emperor muttered to himself. He straightened with a proud air. "I will leave now," he said. "You may stay here and do your thinking or whatever you always do."

And with that, his heavy steps boomed as he exited the pavilion. Pinmei and Yishan pressed tightly against the stone statue, squeezing together. As he passed, a gust of icy air flew out and clawed at them, but he walked by, muttering, without pause. With her one dared peek, Pinmei could see only an opulence of the golden silk dragon robes and black furs.

They waited in silence, the emperor's figure getting smaller and smaller as he walked away, the snow slowly veiling him from view. When he finally disappeared, they waited for the king to depart as well. But the king did not move. He just stood at the pavilion, perhaps watching the emperor as well.

Finally, just when it looked as if Yishan was about to fall asleep from being so still, the king stirred. His footsteps were not stomping, powerful ones like the emperor's, but they too were weighted. They heard his steps come toward the sculpture, but instead of passing by, they stopped and there was a long silence. Yishan and Pinmei looked at each other, puzzled.

"I know you are there," the king said. "You might as well come out."

CHAPTER
35

"How did you know we were here?" Yishan said as they crawled out from behind the statue.

The king gave a small, sad smile, the lantern in his hand casting a dark shadow on his face.

"This used to be my painting studio," he said, waving his hand at the pavilion. "I know every branch and stone here. When I saw the shape of this shadow, I knew it was not right, even though I have not painted in a long while."

"I imagine your ink would just freeze now," Yishan said with a slight undertone of annoyance.

"I stopped long before winter arrived," the king said. "After I sent my son away, painting lost all its joy."

"We know about your son," Yishan said. "Yanna told us."

The king frowned. "Yanna is a good girl," he said, "but she has not yet learned restraint."

"Well, I think you could forgive her for that," Yishan said, "considering she was running around the army camp for you pointlessly."

"Pointlessly?" the king said, only the slightest question in his voice.

"No prisoners here," Yishan answered. "Yanna said they've been sent to the Vast Wall already."

The king bowed his head, and his hand covered his brow.

"Then all is lost," he said, his eyes closing. "What more can he take from me?"

"Who?" Yishan said.

"The emperor, of course," the king said. He shook his head in disgust and sighed, a sound low but filled with fury. "He's a beast, not a man! He could create a sea with all the blood he has spilled. And is still spilling! That Vast Wall is just a vast grave marker."

"What do you mean?" Yishan asked.

"I am told," the king said, sagging like the winter branches weighted by snow, "that the workers are treated worse than slaves and the emperor has the fallen buried under the wall."

Pinmei looked at him in horror.

"But Lady Meng's husband..." Pinmei whispered.

The king nodded, his head hanging with great grief. "And now," he said in a voice that cracked, "my own son."

The wind blew a low, plaintive moan, the beginning note of a lamenting song.

"I knew it was a vain hope to look for him," the king said finally, lifting his head. "But I could not refuse Yanna's offer. I hope she is safe."

"I do too," Pinmei said, and the king's eyes looked directly at her for the first time.

"I think I will soon be having that same wish for both of you as well," the king said, his shoulders straightening as if he were awakening. "Why are you two children here?"

CHAPTER
36

"Do you not realize how dangerous this is?" the king continued. "If the emperor were ever to know you were... What did you hear?"

"We heard you read the Paper of Answers," Yishan told him.

The king drew a sharp breath. "Then you must leave as soon as possible," he said. "The emperor would have you killed just for knowing I have the Paper."

"How do you even have the Paper?" Pinmei asked, her curiosity stronger than her timidity. "I thought it was given away."

"That is a complicated story," the king said. "I am not sure if I even understand it, much less believe it."

"What do you mean?" Yishan asked.

The king hesitated. "Do either of you know the story of how the first king of the City of Bright Moonlight's father turned into a tiger?"

"The Story of the Green Tiger?" Pinmei said instantly. "Of course."

"Well, I don't," Yishan said. "So tell me."

The king waved his hand at Pinmei. "I would be interested in hearing your version of the story," he said.

So Pinmei began.

THE STORY OF THE GREEN TIGER

A long time ago, even before the time of my grandmother, the emperor called all the kings of his land to his Spring Festival celebration. At the palace, he presented to each of the kings a small seed.

"Each one of you is to plant and care for your seed as if it were your kingdom," said the emperor. "At the Moon Festival, you are to bring your plant to me. Those with the best flowers will be rewarded, but if any of you fail to bring me a plant…"

The emperor did not need to finish his sentence. The kings had all thrown themselves into kowtows, each swearing he would return at the Moon Festival with splendid flowers. One by one, they left, each taking his precious seed with him.

The young king of the City of Bright Moonlight returned home to find his father waiting for him. The father had once been a powerful magistrate but had fallen out of favor and was bitterly living at the palace. When the son told him of the emperor's task, the father was excited.

"You must grow the most magnificent flower," the father commanded. "This is your opportunity to return me to power!"

The young king did not disagree and planted the seed with great care in a pot. Faithfully, he watered and waited for the seed to sprout. Nothing grew.

The days turned into weeks and the weeks into months, and still the pot was bare. The king replanted the seed and called the best gardeners of his land to consult. But still nothing grew.

Throughout this, the king's father wore a frown that seemed to become permanent on his face. He had sent spies to neighboring kingdoms and heard rumors of orchids, peonies, and lilies. Yet his son had only a dirt-filled pot. If nothing grew by the Moon Festival, the king's father thought, this chance would be lost and, considering the emperor's ire, perhaps worse.

So when there was still no plant growing in the pot a month before the Moon Festival, the father confronted his son on his nightly stroll through the garden.

"You will have to leave for the Imperial Palace soon," the father said. "And your pot is bare."

The king nodded. In his hands was a piece of paper; the father recognized it as the paper he himself had given him as a wedding gift.

"I've prepared another pot for you," the father said. "In secret, I had the gardener grow a rare moonflower. It is the finest ever seen. You can bring that instead."

The king was silent, and for a long moment, he stared out at the lake before him.

"Thank you, Father, for your consideration," the king said finally. "But I will bring my bare pot."

"You do not understand," the father said impatiently. "The king of the City of Winding River has grown a red peony so bright it looks as if it is on fire. The king of the City of Far Clouds has an orchid with the fragrance of a sweet apple. All the kings will have flowers in their pots. What will you say to the emperor when you have none?"

"I will tell the emperor I tried my best to grow his seed," the king said, "yet nothing grew. I must tell the truth."

"Are you crazy?" the father said. "Do you know what the emperor will do? He will take away your kingdom! He might even execute you for the insult!"

"That may be," the king said. "But I cannot lie. It would be found out eventually, so I must go with my own pot."

"I can make sure no one finds out," the father said. "I will have the gardener and his family killed and throw all who may know into the dungeon."

The young king blanched at his father's words and looked at the paper in his hands.

"Father," the king said, without looking up, "I will bring my bare pot."

"Don't be a fool!" his father snapped. "You must bring a flower or I will never return to power!"

The king gave a wry smile at those last words, a smile the father did not understand. As the paper in the king's hand flapped like a nervous butterfly, the father grew angrier.

"Why are you looking at that paper?" the father growled. "What are you reading?"

The king looked up with reluctance. He glanced at the moon and its reflection wavering in the lake, the murky green water rippling in uneasy waves.

"It says, 'Three things cannot long be hidden: the sun, the moon,'" the king said slowly, holding the paper for his father to see, "'and the truth.'"

At this, the father gasped. "It is that accursed paper that is giving you this idiotic advice!" he cried. "You are listening more to that infernal piece of paper than your own father!"

The father gave an infuriated roar and grabbed the paper from his son, seizing it with such force that he fell backward into the lake, shattering the reflection of the moon. The paper slipped from his fingers and, almost as if it were a fish, floated over his face. The father thrashed and flailed, clawing to peel the paper from his face. But as he struggled to lift the paper, he realized he no longer had hands!

His hands had turned to paws and his skin was wet fur of the same color as the murky water. His clothes writhed around him until they finally twisted off. And when at last the paper fell away, he knew his face had changed as well. The young king gaped in shock, and the father was only able to see why when the reflection of the moon returned to the lake. He had turned into a tiger!

"Wait!" Yishan interrupted. "I thought the first king of the City of Bright Moonlight exiled his father."

"He did," Pinmei said. "He had to. When his father turned into a tiger, the first king couldn't let him stay in the city. He was too dangerous. So his father was exiled."

"So it was as a tiger that he was exiled?" Yishan said, scratching his head and looking up as if trying to read a lost memory in the night sky. "I guess that would make sense…"

"If you believe the story, that is," the king interjected. "There are many parts I find doubtful."

"But what does this have to do with the Paper?" Pinmei asked. "The Paper turned the first king's father into a tiger, but that was long before the Paper was given away. How can you have it now?"

"It was my father, the former king of the City of Bright Moonlight, who gave the Paper away over sixty years ago," the king said. "After he abdicated and became quite old, he returned to the palace with the Paper and a strange story."

Pinmei looked at Yishan, but he did not meet her eyes. Instead, he was gazing upward. Another star was flying across the sky, making a silver scratch on the black-lacquered night. Pinmei frowned and turned back to the king.

"Does it have something to do with the Green Tiger?" she asked.

"Yes," the king said. "I suppose it could be considered a new part of the Green Tiger story."

"A new part of the Story of the Green Tiger?" Pinmei repeated, giving Yishan a sharp nudge. He glanced at her apologetically. "I didn't know there was a new part. Please, Your Majesty. I would like to hear the story."

THE NEW PART OF THE STORY OF THE GREEN TIGER

My father, in his old age, had taken to traveling in disguise to enjoy the pleasures of common life. One night, on one of his trips, he decided to go for a night walk and found himself by a lake so large and black he could not tell where the water ended and the sky began. In fact, he would not have even known it was a lake at all if it wasn't for the giant moon reflected in the water.

It was a beautiful sight, and he sat down to admire it. As he rested, he began to hear a strange sound.

A loud splashing echoed in the air, and a giant beast burst from the lake as if ripping through a paper moon. The beast crawled out of the lake, and when it reached the shore, it panted and gasped, exhausted. My father said he had never seen a more wretched creature.

"A hard journey, was it not?" a voice said. There was an old man speaking to the beast. He was a man with a long gray beard who my father insisted came from nowhere. "He just appeared," my father said.

The miserable beast did nothing but give a low, pitiful moan.

"Do you wonder why I am here?" the old man said. "Or why you were finally able to free yourself from your prison of the well to this lake?"

The beast finally raised his head, and my father gasped. It was a tiger!

"Your son did a great service for us," the man said, waving his hand toward the moon. "And his dying wish was to have you return. It is only now, after you have reached your fifth Year of the Tiger without creating harm, that we can fulfill his wish."

My father watched, mesmerized, as the old man took a paper out of his sleeve. He dipped it in the water and bent over the trembling tiger.

"I fear I will regret this," the man said. "You do not seem to learn from your past mistakes."

And with that, he placed the wet paper on the animal's face. The tiger shuddered, and my father watched as the old man stood up and turned toward the water. Strangely, as the old man stepped onto the lake, he did not sink but walked straight onto the path of moonlight reflected on the water.

When my father looked back at the tiger, the beast was reaching for the paper on his face...but the beast's claws had transformed into fingers! And when the paper was finally peeled off, the tiger was a man!

The man who had been a beast stood, stared at the departing figure walking toward the moon, and then dropped the paper as if it were diseased. The paper floated in the air like a white butterfly and landed in my father's lap. The man saw my father holding the paper and gave an inhuman roar and leaped in the opposite direction. "He ran on his hands and feet, as if he were still an animal," my father said. "I knew who he was and what he had been. He had been the Green Tiger."

"The Green Tiger!" Pinmei gasped. "The first king's father turned back into a man? He could be the emperor!"

"No, no," the king said. "That's impossible. How could the first king's father, be him man or beast, be alive for so long? The first king was generations before even my own father's time. For the first king's father to be alive, he would have to be an immortal, and we all know the emperor is not an immortal."

"At least, not yet," Yishan added darkly. He was no longer distracted by the sky and was, instead, staring intensely at the king.

"Then your father's story..." Pinmei began.

"My father was very old and often mixed dreams with reality," the king said. "Once he dreamed he was a butterfly, and when he awoke, he thought he was a butterfly dreaming he was man. There's no doubt this story was confused as well."

"But the Paper," Pinmei insisted. "You have the Paper."

"Part of his story was probably true," the king agreed, "for it *is* the Paper of Answers. I spent many long years learning how to read it."

"And now you use that knowledge to help the emperor?" Yishan said, and the anger in his tone surprised Pinmei. "Even if the emperor is not the Green Tiger, he is just as bad! He's using whatever you tell him to gain more power, kill more people, and now live forever! How dare you use the Paper for him?"

"What would you have me do?" the king said. "I am a prisoner in my own palace, and spies surround me. How could I do anything else?"

Yishan glared and the king looked back defiantly, almost as if he were the small child and Yishan the adult. The wind whined, its cold breath freezing them into two scowling statues. Stroking Amah's bracelet desperately, Pinmei glanced from one to the other. The smooth jade soothed her cold-cracked fingers, and she was surprised when she heard her own voice speaking.

"Your Majesty," Pinmei said, her quiet words loud in the silence, "I did not finish my story. May I tell you the end?"

THE END OF THE STORY OF THE GREEN TIGER

After the shock of his father's transformation was over, the young king looked at the moonflower his father had prepared. It was, indeed, a beautiful plant. The king gazed at it and looked at his own pot, full of only black dirt, and shook his head.

On the day of the Moon Festival, the king of the City of Bright Moonlight arrived at the Imperial Palace with his bare pot. As he passed each gorgeous peony and peach blossom, every elegant chrysanthe-mum and lily, he heard horrified murmurs.

And the dismay was justified. For when the emperor saw the king's pot, his face turned as black as iron.

"What is this?" demanded the emperor. "A bare pot? Whose is this?"

"It is mine," the young king said as he prostrated himself on the floor.

"I will strip you of your kingdom for your insult!" the emperor bellowed. "How dare you!"

"I am sorry, Your Exalted Majesty," the king said, flattening himself even lower to the ground. "I tried my best to grow your seed, but nothing grew."

"You could not grow a simple seed? How incompe-tent are you?" the emperor barked.

He looked at the king before him and the vibrant flowers surrounding him. Orange and vermillion, magenta and gold—the colors blazed like flames.

"Tell me," the emperor said in a slightly different tone, "do you not have a better excuse than that? Did not your unskilled gardener destroy the plant? Or perhaps one of your rival kings poisoned your soil?"

"No, Your Exalted Majesty," the king said. "I was just unable to grow your seed."

"Answer carefully, young king," the emperor said in a menacing tone, "for your life may depend on your answer. Who is to blame for this empty pot?"

The king raised his head. His face was white, but he said without hesitation, "I am."

The room gasped, and all expected the emperor to call his guards to drag the king away. But, instead, the emperor smiled and stood and motioned for the young king to stand.

"All bow to him!" the emperor ordered. "Bow to the greatest king in my empire!"

The other kings were confused, but they all lowered their heads.

"Only the bravest and most virtuous of men would dare to bring me a bare pot," the emperor said, "as well as refuse to blame another. You are a man of great honor."

"I do not understand," the king said.

"No one could have grown a flower from the seeds I gave," the emperor said. "I boiled them."

When Pinmei finished her story, the silence returned, but it was a gentle quiet, without resentment. For a long moment, the king looked out, past the stone sculpture to the frozen lake. Then he bowed his head to Yishan.

"You are right," he said in a low voice. "If my ancestors knew how I have helped the emperor, they would be ashamed."

As he raised his head, Pinmei glimpsed his haunted eyes and saw how broken he was by worry and regret. She forgot he was king and touched his arm gently. He looked at her, and his anguished eyes softened. He patted her hand with gratitude, the soft snowflakes landing on them like resting stars.

A strange twittering filled the air. Pinmei's face yanked skyward. It was Lady Meng's swallow! And running in the distance, Lady Meng!

They rushed to her as she clutched at them. "Yanna sent me!" she gasped. "Told me...the emperor...soldiers...guards..."

There was a *twang!* in the air and a high-pitched shriek. *Thud!* Something fell from the sky. Pinmei looked down. At Yishan's feet was a mussel with the tip of a soldier's arrow in it.

CHAPTER

37

Yishan grabbed the fallen mussel and tossed away the arrow. "We need to leave now!" he said, looking at the king.

"Come with me," the king said, nodding. "Quickly!"

He led them off the curving path deeper into the garden. In the distance, they could hear the guards shouting, their feet stomping on the snow-covered walkway. The king pulled them behind a giant, rough-hewn statue, and they all stopped. The stone wall of the garden lay in front of them.

"What..." Yishan began.

"Shh," the king said. He'd taken off his gloves and was running his bare palms over the stones. "Here it is," he said in triumph. In the light of his lantern, Pinmei could see he had been looking for an indentation in the wall that was like a...handle? The king pushed with both hands on one of the stones.

They all stared as part of the wall moved! It was a secret door!

The king urged them out. "You must run," he said to them all. "You must leave the city at once. They may not follow you outside the gates of the Outer City."

"KaiJae," Lady Meng said, grabbing his hands, "will you be all right?"

"It is all of you I am worried about," he said, his face shadowed with a darkness beyond that of the night. "Here I am, casting you out of the Inner City, and I have nothing to help protect you except..."

He let go of Lady Meng's hands and reached into his robe. He turned to Pinmei. "Take this," he said, handing her the Paper of Answers.

"That's the...the..." Pinmei said, alarm overwhelming her.

"Yes," the king said. "Perhaps its power will protect you."

"But what about you?" Pinmei sputtered. "When the emperor comes…"

"When he comes, I will have no answers to give him," the king said, looking at Yishan, "and I will no longer dishonor my ancestors by helping such a villain."

"But…the emperor! Without the Paper…" Pinmei said again.

"I have nothing I need to cling to," the king said with surprising calmness. He raised his head and straightened, letting the moon bathe him with silver light.

"Except your life!" Pinmei said. Did the king realize what he was doing? "The emperor might kill you!"

The king put his hands on Pinmei's shoulders. "Thank you, my small friend," he said to her, "for reminding me there are worse things than death."

There were loud shouts and the sound of heavy footsteps coming closer.

"Go!" the king said, pushing Pinmei and the others. And with a vicious yank, he closed the door.

CHAPTER

38

Pinmei shoved the Paper in her sleeve and looked at Lady Meng and Yishan, their blank faces mirroring her own. They needed to go, but which way? Without the swallow, how would they know? Behind the wall, a loud shout rang out. Without a word, Yishan grabbed Pinmei's hand and ran.

Lady Meng followed, and they skidded and stumbled in panic on the snow-covered streets. Up a twisting alley, down a narrow lane—where was the gate out? Were they even going in the right direction? As they kept running, the night grew colder and colder and the wind bit their faces. How many roads were there in the Outer City? It was a cruel maze, with every corner taunting them.

Pinmei did not know how long they wandered, half running and half staggering through the piles of snow and frozen stone streets. Pinmei's feet lost all feeling, and her legs threatened to go limp with each step. As they turned a corner, she grabbed Lady Meng's hand and felt it shiver with cold and exhaustion. Where was the gate?

The blackness of the sky began to lighten and an old peddler came out of a doorway, the creaking of his cart echoing in the silence of the upcoming dawn. Yishan bounded toward him, almost grabbing him.

"The gate out of the city!" Yishan demanded. "Where is it?"

The peddler stared at him, openmouthed, but before he could even make a movement with his hand, there was another noise that made them all turn around.

"Halt!" a voice in the distance yelled. *A soldier!* He was alone, but he wouldn't be for long, for he turned his head and shouted, "They're here! I found them!"

Yishan yelped and leaped over the peddler's cart, Pinmei and Lady Meng close behind him. They turned down one alleyway and then another. The winding roads hid them from view, but they could hear the loud stomping of soldiers in the streets.

Lady Meng pounded on the door of the nearest house. "Please," she said. "Let us in!"

No answer.

Yishan banged on the door of the next house, and Pinmei the next. They ran down the street, knocking and pleading. Scared eyes peeked through curtains that were quickly drawn, and each door stayed silent and shut.

Pinmei felt herself sobbing. Every part of her was trembling with cold, exhaustion, and despair. Lady Meng drooped like a dying flower, and even Yishan's pace had slowed. Yet the sounds of soldiers were getting louder. Closer. Closer. "Please help us," Pinmei begged in a whisper to the wind. "Please!"

A faint voice called out. "Here," it said. "Over here!"

As if clouds had uncovered the moon, a soft light streamed toward them from a gate down the lane. The large figure of a woman beckoned to them. Pinmei felt relief flood through her, the waves of gratitude carrying her in reckless abandon, as they crashed through the open door.

CHAPTER
39

"Thank you!" Pinmei gasped.

"Shh!" the woman said, shutting the door. Broad and strong, she was obviously a servant, but when she raised the lantern, Pinmei gasped again, this time in surprise. For while the woman's eyes were kind, her face was horribly scarred—the skin as rough as the outside of an oyster shell. But the woman blew out the flame, and she was just a shadow in the thin darkness of early dawn.

Pinmei looked around and saw they were in the outer courtyard of a rich mansion. The high walls hid them from view, but there were few places to hide. She gulped. The soldiers were almost there. She could hear echoing noises coming closer—the stomping boots, the bangs as the soldiers forced open doors not opened quickly enough, the shouted questions. Lady Meng and Yishan crouched next to her, and when the soldiers struck at the door of the gate, they all clutched one another.

"Open, by order of the emperor!" the soldier barked.

"Shh," the woman said again to them. She pushed them out of sight of the door and, with an unhurried pace, went to the gate.

"The children!" the soldier growled. "Are they here?"

"Who? What children?" the woman asked. Her tone was placid and calm, but Pinmei saw that her hand gripped the door tightly.

"The spying children! Are they here?" the man spat impatiently. He made as if to force his way through the door, but the woman stood firm and blocked his entry, her hulking figure as large as his.

"Sir, this is the House of Wu," she said, as if talking to a small child. "Surely you know my masters are highly favored by the emperor."

The soldier froze.

"If my masters were to complain about the annoyance caused by his soldier..." the woman said, drawing herself up to her fullest height to gaze directly into his eyes.

"Uh, yes," the soldier said, lowering his arm as well as his tone. "Of course, the honorable House of Wu is above any suspicion. I was just checking to make sure the household was not bothered by these, uh, young nuisances."

"How kind," the woman said. "We have not been bothered, except by the wind that is now coming through this door."

"Uh, yes," the soldier said again, bowing as he retreated from the doorway. The woman shut the door before he even raised his head. Then she stood against the door like a propped tree, and they all waited for the heavy steps of the soldier to fade.

"There," the woman said, finally looking at them. "That takes care of them. Now, how should we take care of you?"

CHAPTER

40

"I think food first," the woman said with a smile. "Come."

She led them through another gate to the inner court-yard and past the side hall, her finger pressed to her lips for silence. Despite her size, she walked noiselessly, and they followed her to the kitchen. The warmth of the room made them stumble as if they were wading in honey. She led them to the stove and began to spoon rice porridge into bowls, its steam issuing like a sighing breath.

"Eat," the woman said, holding out a bowl, her large fin-gers almost completely hiding the design of a painted monkey.

"Thank you," Lady Meng said, taking it. "We..."

"It matters not," said the woman, pressing another bowl toward Yishan.

"But…" Pinmei said as the woman held out a third bowl. The rich smell of the porridge was intoxicating, and its hot mist made a translucent cloud around the woman, softening her many scars. "Who are you?"

The woman laughed. "I am just a servant in the House of Wu," she said. "Of no importance, I assure you."

"Your masters must be very kind," Lady Meng said.

The woman laughed again. "Oh no," she said. "They are quite the opposite, in fact."

"Then…" Pinmei said. "Won't you get in trouble?"

"Most probably," the woman said, nodding.

"But…" Pinmei hesitated as Yishan gave her a pointed look. She didn't want to be cast out, but she needed to understand. "Why are you helping us?"

The woman looked at Pinmei, smiled sadly, and lifted the lantern up to her face.

"Do you know what kind of scars these are?" the woman asked her.

With the light on them, Pinmei could see they were all shaped like small, sharp slivers.

"Are they…" Pinmei said slowly, almost in disbelief, "Scars of Stingy Rice?"

"Yes," the old woman said, nodding. "You know the story."

"What is the story?" Lady Meng said, looking from Pinmei to the woman.

"Ah, I'm no good at storytelling," the old woman said. She looked at Pinmei. "You tell it."

THE STORY OF THE SCARS OF STINGY RICE

There was once a rich lord who had always been wealthy. Perhaps one reason he had so much money was because he never gave to the poor. During times of famine or drought, he never gave one spoonful of rice to a starving child, even though his jars were overflowing with grains. In fact, he flaunted his fortune. Every day, equally wealthy friends were invited to dine on Jade Tree Chicken and Silk Squash Noodles while the hungry stood outside on the street by his house.

When the rich lord turned sixty, he decided he would throw his most lavish banquet.

"I have seen the Year of the Monkey five times!" the lord said with pride. "I shall have a celebration to match such an auspicious event!"

So he ordered the slaughter of a half-dozen pigs and a flock of ducks and arranged for the most luxurious long-life robe to be made for himself. As he inspected the fabrics, a blue silk pleased him so much he decided not only to have a robe made of it, but also to use it to line the road to his house. *It will be a fitting pathway to my home*, he thought.

However, the road outside the house was not in good condition, and the delicate silk wrinkled over the many cracks and holes in the street.

"This will not do!" the lord roared, and he commanded his servants to even out the road by filling the gaps with uncooked rice.

"But won't people try to take the rice?" a servant protested.

"Have anyone who tries arrested," the lord growled. "No beggar is to steal even a single grain!"

So the servants did as they were told, to the horrified awe of the people on the street. More than once, hungry beggars attempted to grab a handful of rice. But the lord's servants promptly had them thrown in jail.

When the servants finished their work and the silk lay smoothly on the road, an old man came walking down it, leaning on a stick. As he walked, the grains of rice made a crunching noise under his feet. He stopped in front of the lord's house, raising his head to breathe in the delicious smells of the upcoming banquet.

"Eight Treasure Duck," the old man murmured to himself, licking his lips as is if he were tasting the savory flavors. "Lion Head Pork Meatballs…"

"Away from here!" a servant cried. "Away!"

"Please," the old man said, stretching out an arm, "your master is having a grand feast. Surely you can spare a small bit for me?"

"Go!" the servant yelled, waving a stick.

"Perhaps," the old man said, "I could just take a few grains of this rice, then?"

And the old man reached down and plucked some rice from underneath the silk.

"Thief!" the servants bellowed, calling for the others. "Thief!"

With the other servants came the lord of the house, who was furious to be called away from his party.

"You worthless body," the lord screeched. "How dare you try to steal from me!"

He turned to his servants. "Beat him until every part of him is bruised and broken!"

The servants lifted their sticks, but instead of cowering, the old man stood calmly. The servants hesitated, but the lord snapped angrily, "Do as I say! *Now!*"

They began striking him. The old man remained unmoved, but after the first few blows, the lord began to howl with pain. "Stop!" he cried. "Stop!" For each time they hit the old man, it was the lord who felt it. He collapsed, whimpering, on the ground.

The old man continued to stand. "Goodbye," he said to the stunned crowds. "I cannot say I enjoyed your company, but I shall leave you something to remember me by."

He walked down the silk pathway. When he reached the end of the silk, he turned to look at the staring servants and the sniveling lord and bent down. Then, as if breathing out a cloud, he blew.

The silk lifted and waved, and the hundreds of thousands of grains of rice rose into the air. They whipped up into the sky and flew toward the lord and his servants like a swarm of mosquitoes. They cringed, but the rice fell upon them without mercy, melting into their skin. Immediately, their faces and bodies were covered with hundreds of white scars—all shaped like the grains of rice that had rained upon them. They shouted in dismay and shock and looked for the old man. But the old man was nowhere in sight. Unlike the scars, he had faded away and was never seen again.

"Yes, yes," the woman said. "It was just like that. The old story had been whispered down through the House of Wu for generations, but none believed it happened or, if it did, that it could happen again. But it did, and almost exactly the same way—except it was my mistress and she had a silk the green color of jade." She shook her head. "How they love their jade."

"Then, did you...you..." Pinmei faltered.

The scarred woman sat down heavily and looked at her empty hands, her bell-shaped figure an iron shadow in the light of the lantern.

"I was named after a great hero, you know?" she said softly. "And I always wanted to be the same. And back then, it seemed like I was. For I was as mighty as any man and just as proud."

The fire in the cookstove flickered and wavered, making

noises like the opening of a crumpled paper. Outside, the black sky began to thin.

"But that was only on the outside," the scarred woman said, her huge shoulders slumping. "Inside, I was weak and cowardly. I was too scared not to follow the commands of my masters. I beat the beggar."

The woman lifted her head. Night was fading, and faint gauze ribbons of light stretched through the window toward them.

"When I heard you calling for help," she said, putting her hand on Pinmei's cheek, "I knew this was a chance to make amends for my past shame. I could not be a coward again. You have thanked me, but it is I who thank you."

Outside, the sun rose and the soft light streamed in. The gray glow of morning did nothing to disguise the scars on the woman's face, but they could see the gentle look in her eyes.

Pinmei felt tears beginning to sting. The woman's hands were warm and wrinkled, touching hers with a tenderness so much like Amah's.

"You are tired," the woman said. "Come and rest."

Pinmei let herself be led to a large pillow next to the stove, its heat bathing her in warmth. Her weary legs and arms were limp and all but collapsed onto the padding.

"Who was the hero you were named after?" Pinmei asked, her eyes already beginning to close.

"The great Haiyi," the woman said. "He was one of my ancestors."

"But he..." Pinmei began, but a yawn interrupted her words.

"Shhh," the woman said. "It matters not."

Pinmei's words and fears melted in the warmth of the woman's kindness, and she did not try to say more. She was so tired.

"Now," the woman said, "just rest."

So Pinmei did.

CHAPTER
41

Who should he call? He did not know if he was in the sky, the earth, or the sea. It did not really matter. Whomever he called, someone would come. But, before this, he had last been swimming in the lake, so he would call the Sea King.

But how to reach him?

None had heard his cries. However, even to his own ears, his bellows seemed muffled. Perhaps, outside this golden emptiness, his sounds were stifled to silence.

He would have to send a message directly.

The Black Tortoise hesitated. Was it the only way?

It would not hurt him and he would heal immediately, he knew. But still, it was...unpleasant.

He looked around again and saw only the bare brilliance. He twisted his arms and legs, feeling the emptiness.

Yes, it was the only way. Very well.

He stuck out his tongue, stretching it as long as he could. Then, with a powerful snap, *he bit off his tongue with his own teeth.*

It fell on the gold ground, only to bound back up as if springing from a cushion. It began to roll and twist, lengthening and thinning, until it looked like a long black cord knotted at one end. Finally, it made a sinuous curve toward him, the bulbous knot resembling a head.

The Black Tortoise blew on it, a calm, controlled gust of air. The black coil trembled. From its knotted head, two eyes opened. Something tiny, like a frayed string, flicked from its mouth.

His tongue had turned into a snake.

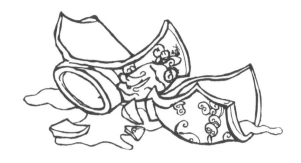

CHAPTER
42

"What is this? Who is that?" a sharp voice shouted. Pinmei woke up as if she had been slapped. She opened her eyes and saw Haiyi, the servant, cringing in the corner, and two richly dressed figures standing over her. As one of them—a puny man heaped with lavish fur and silk—turned to glare at her, Pinmei could see they were as scarred as the servant. Their opulent clothing, elaborate and glittering, could not hide their disfigurement, and their unpleasant expressions made them hideous. Pinmei knew immediately these were the masters of the House of Wu.

"You're always helping little beggars to our property!"

screeched the other of them—the woman—as ornate gold pins in her hair shook. She threw a bowl at the servant. It broke against the wall next to Haiyi's head, the cold soup splashing everywhere. "Rice porridge! Dumplings! I've seen you!"

"I've only given my portion!" Haiyi protested, not even bothering to wipe the liquid from her face.

"And now you even let them into our house!" shrieked the man, grabbing the broomstick leaning against the wall. He raised it wickedly, his silk sleeve falling to reveal his hairy, wiry arm. "How dare you!"

"No, please, master!" Haiyi begged, cowering. "Please!"

But before the man could lower the stick, Pinmei rushed forward.

"*Stop!*" she screamed, placing herself between the man and Haiyi. "Stop it!"

The man sputtered in shock and outrage, and Pinmei could only stare back. He looked more like an animal than a man. His rough-skinned face was purple with rage, and the veins in his eyes bulged like tiny red worms. Pinmei paled, but she did not move.

"You want a taste of the stick too, you little beggar?" the man sneered, spitting drops of saliva.

"I'm not a beggar!" Pinmei said, raising her voice to

hide its quavering. Without thinking, she took the jade bracelet off her arm and held it up.

The green circle seemed to glow. Vibrant and clear, the sunlight glided through it, making an emerald ring of light on the wall. Even from a distance, all could see the bracelet's exquisite beauty and were, for a moment, stunned into silence.

Yishan and Lady Meng, awakened by the noise, came in from the other room, but Pinmei barely saw them. Her eyes were fixed on the masters of the House of Wu. Their heads looked small sticking out of their extravagant fur collars, but their mouths were wide open.

Their expressions shifted, and Pinmei watched their shock transform into desire. The woman's eyes glittered like black beetles in her ravaged face, and the man licked his lips as if hungry. Pinmei swallowed.

"Do you want this?" Pinmei said, holding the bracelet higher. The polished stone glinted, and Pinmei felt as if she were offering a treat to rabid dogs. "Then promise you will never hit her again and you'll leave us alone!"

Almost panting with greed, the two quickly nodded and Pinmei slowly held out the jade bracelet. They pounced toward her, and Pinmei felt a sharp, sad pain in her chest. How often had she clung to this bracelet? The jade, so pure and clear—like Amah's voice waking her in the morning. And the cool, strong stone—like Amah's hand steadying her across the ice. Could she really let these . . . these beasts have it? Her hand tightened around the bracelet and its perfect circle pressed back into her fingers as if resisting. *Amah would want me to*, Pinmei thought. She closed her eyes and released the bracelet.

The couple clutched it together, pushing each other away to examine it closer. Pinmei turned away. She knelt beside Haiyi, reached into her sleeve, and gave the scarred servant her handkerchief to wipe the spilled soup from her face. Yishan and Lady Meng quickly joined them.

"Pinmei, you . . ." Yishan said to her with admiration. "You were really great."

"Was I?" Pinmei said faintly, and she found that she was trembling. "I didn't think. . . . I just wanted to make them stop."

"I'm sorry you gave away your bracelet," Lady Meng said, looking in distaste at the masters of the House of Wu. They were inspecting the bracelet at the window, the man biting into it to test the stone.

"You're a brave girl," Haiyi said, lifting her face from the cloth. "Much braver than . . ."

The other three gasped. Haiyi stopped at the sound and saw they were staring at her.

"Your...your face!" Pinmei breathed. "Your scars are gone!"

It was true. The raised white scars had disappeared. Instead, the woman's face was as smooth as the inside of a seashell.

"My scars?" Haiyi said, and her fingers stroked the even skin on her face in disbelief. She opened her other hand and, from Pinmei's handkerchief, hundreds of rice grains fell onto the floor like a sudden rain shower.

But it wasn't Pinmei's handkerchief! Pinmei cried out in astonishment. It was the Paper of Answers!

CHAPTER
43

Pinmei had given Haiyi the Paper of Answers by mistake! And it had wiped away her scars! How could that be possible? But it was—the skin of Haiyi's face was even and unblemished, and a puddle of uncooked rice lay at her feet.

"What is going on over there?" said one of the hideous masters of the House of Wu, alerted by Pinmei's yelp. His beady eyes glittered and the woman raised her head as if smelling a feast. "What are you doing?"

They scampered over, leaping over furniture in their eagerness, but stopped abruptly when they saw their servant.

"Y-your scars..." the man stuttered. "How did you..."

"You wiped them away!" the woman shrieked. "It must be that cloth! Give it to me!"

Before the other could even shout, they fell upon their servant, snatching the Paper from her hands. Without hesitating, they began to rub their faces vigorously, each after the other.

But when they raised their hands to touch their skin, their scars had not disappeared. Instead, their faces were puckering and shriveling, their fur collars almost swallowing their heads. No, it wasn't their collars! The man and woman were sprouting fur! Their faces, arms, and legs were covered with dark brown hair the color of rotting wood. And it wasn't just their faces—their whole bodies were shrinking too! They grew smaller and smaller until their fine silk capes and robes and hairpins fell on the stone floor and covered them. Four dark hands reached out and pushed the silks open, and two small furry heads thrust out. The others cried in shock.

The masters of the House of Wu had turned into monkeys!

The two monkeys glowered, their eyes full of fury. Pinmei could only gape, her mouth a round circle, her head dizzy with astonishment.

Haiyi stood and grabbed the broom. "Shoo! Shoo!" she said. Yishan opened the door and Haiyi swept at the monkeys. "Out!" she scolded. "Out!"

The monkeys chattered angrily, spitting and clawing, but their former servant was persistent, pushing and shoving with the broom until both monkeys were out the door. Finally, the monkeys scampered into the snow-covered courtyard and over the wall, sputtering outraged noises.

Pinmei continued to stare at them, sinewy black shadows against the snow. Before they disappeared behind the wall, one turned and shook its fist at them, a brilliant green flashing from its hairy arm. Yishan slammed the door.

"Monkeys are always such a nuisance," he said, shaking his head.

CHAPTER
44

"Well, that was unexpected," Haiyi said with a broad smile. Now that her scars were gone, Pinmei could see her wide, pleasant face, dimpled with laughter. The woman swept away the broken bowl with a flourish, almost dancing with the broom. Still smiling, she looked at the others. "And what are your plans now, my friends?"

"First, we have to get out of the city," Yishan said. "How far are we from the Outer City gate?"

"Oh, very close!" the woman said, pausing in her sweeping to pick up the Paper from the floor. She handed it to Pinmei with another smile. "The emperor left this morning, while you slept. The emperor has left orders to have you killed if you are found, of course, but when he heard you were children, he didn't feel he needed to waste any more time or men on you. I'm sure we could sneak you out easily now."

"After we leave the city, I am going to the Vast Wall to find my husband," Lady Meng said.

Haiyi stopped sweeping and looked at Lady Meng, her eyes full of sympathy and dismay. She opened her mouth to say something, but Lady Meng's head rose defiantly. She looked out the window, her figure shrouded in a gauze curtain of cold white light. Haiyi closed her mouth and looked at the children. "And you two?" she said finally. "Surely you will not be going to the Vast Wall as well?"

Pinmei shook her head, but neither she nor Yishan gave any other answer. The dragon's pearl was not the Luminous Stone. Amah was not here. They had come to the City of Bright Moonlight for nothing. What were they going to do now? As Haiyi swept, the pieces of the broken bowl clinked together and made a hollow sound.

"You are welcome to stay here as long as you wish," Haiyi said. She lifted a large pot of soup onto the stove and looked at her reflection. "I was never a beauty," she said, touching her face, "but now I would not trade with the goddess Nuwa."

"That's good, because you'd have to have a fish tail," Yishan said almost absently as he gazed at Lady Meng, "which would better if you were in the sea instead of—"

"Yishan!" Pinmei said, sitting up. "Do you remember what the emperor said to the king about the stone? How the king would understand if he went to Sea Bottom?"

"Yes," Yishan said, turning toward her. "I don't remember everything, but I do remember that. So?"

"I think," Pinmei said, "the emperor was saying that the Luminous Stone is at Sea Bottom."

Yishan stared at her, a grin growing on his face.

"You're right!" Yishan said. "That must be where the Luminous Stone—whatever it is—must be! Let's go there next!"

"But..." Pinmei faltered, "Sea Bottom is just part of Amah's stories. Could we really go... How could we get there?"

Lady Meng looked up. "I know how," she said quietly.

CHAPTER
45

The snake's eyes, like deep dark pinpricks, gazed at the Black Tortoise. It stretched toward the tortoise as if longing to embrace it.

The tortoise snapped, and the snake arched back, chastised.

Go to the Sea King, *the tortoise ordered,* and tell him I need help.

The snake nodded, its tongue flicking with eagerness. Without a sound, it turned and began to slither away with surprising speed.

The tortoise fixed his gaze upon it, cherishing the only relief in that brilliant landscape. He watched the black snake crawl and glide until it became a thin silk thread in the distance and disappeared.

CHAPTER
46

"We need to wait for BaiMa," Lady Meng said.

They were outside the city gates, safe from view. They had left the House of Wu quickly, Haiyi urging everything from dumplings to furs on them. "I don't think my masters will need them anymore," Haiyi had said with a small, mischievous smile. Instead, Lady Meng had traded her fine clothes for the coarse garb of the servant herself, and Pinmei and Yishan had thrown various robes and cloaks over their colorful clothing. Leaving separately, they had attracted little attention, and the gates had been easy to exit, just as Haiyi had predicted.

"The horse?" Yishan asked. "But he was put in the palace stable. Surely he couldn't..."

But before Yishan could continue, Lady Meng put two fingers in her mouth and whistled. It was a clear, lilting noise, like the sound of a bamboo flute.

In answer came the high whinny of a horse. BaiMa, as if he had been waiting, galloped toward them from around the bend in the wall. When he reached them, he snorted as if laughing.

"I asked Yanna to let him out of the city gates before I left," Lady Meng said, smiling at their astonishment.

Yishan flung off the borrowed gray cloak and laughed. Pinmei smiled too. Without thinking, she reached to rub the bracelet that was no longer there. Lady Meng saw her.

"I'm sorry you gave away your bracelet," Lady Meng said. "If I had my jewelry here, I could give you many more—gold as well as jade."

Pinmei gave Lady Meng a small smile, the emptiness on her wrist heavier than any gold.

"Jade and gold?" scoffed Yishan. "Who needs that?"

And with a flourish, he pulled a thread out of his fraying sleeve and tied it around Pinmei's wrist. "I present to you this magnificent bracelet of thread," he said in a playful tone as he bowed. "Wear it with pride, for it is priceless!"

Pinmei laughed. "Stop teasing me," she said, but the red string did look nice, and her wrist somehow felt less bare. Despite his joking manner, Pinmei knew Yishan had given it to her in kindness, and it made her feel as if she were drinking a warm cup of tea. She smiled.

Lady Meng looked at them wistfully.

"I wish I had had a bracelet like that to give to my husband," she said sadly.

Yishan turned to Lady Meng and bowed his head. "I wish I could have given him one," he said.

Pinmei watched the two of them, aware something was being said she did not understand. But before she could say anything, Lady Meng raised her head and said, "Shall we be off, then?"

They climbed onto BaiMa's back, and Lady Meng urged the horse forward.

"Aren't we going to the road?" Pinmei asked as BaiMa trotted onto unmarked snow.

"We don't need it," Lady Meng said, clicking at BaiMa to start him galloping. "We're going to the sea."

CHAPTER
47

BaiMa sliced through the air, the wind making Pinmei's braid a stroke of black ink on the paper white of the sky. Time and distance melted together in a blur of silver, and when they stopped, she felt as if they had arrived in another world. For before them, glittering with the cold, hard, sharp sparkle of a diamond, was the sea.

"It's frozen," Pinmei whispered. "The sea is frozen."

They stood for a moment in awe.

"This is not right," Yishan said. "Something is wrong. For the sea to freeze..."

But he stopped, for Lady Meng had slid off the horse. "We will part here," she said to them.

"You're leaving us?" Pinmei gasped.

"I am glad to have spent this time with you both," she said. "But I must find my husband."

"But then how will we…" Pinmei stopped, embarrassed by her selfishness.

Lady Meng smiled at her and looked at Yishan. "I know," she said, "how capable you are." She opened her hand and held it toward him.

Yishan reached deep into his sleeve and fished out his handkerchief, his chopsticks, and, finally, the dark brown mussel. It was tightly closed, with only the smallest indentation as evidence that it had been struck by the arrow. Yishan handed the mussel to Lady Meng.

Lady Meng turned toward the silent sea. The arched frozen waves stretched toward her like yearning arms and, for a long moment, she gazed at them. Then she threw the mussel. As it bounced, it made a clinking noise like a small bell, then became a dark dot rolling in the distance.

"Just follow it," Lady Meng said, looking at them. "BaiMa will know the rest."

"You're not going to take BaiMa?" Pinmei asked.

"No, you'll need him," Lady Meng said, "and I will not. And considering where I am going, he would only draw unnecessary attention to me."

Pinmei tried to picture Lady Meng, refined and graceful, among the horrors of the Vast Wall and found herself shuddering. Lady Meng looked at her with affection.

"Do not worry for me, Pinmei," she said. "I must follow my path."

Pinmei nodded. "I wish I could be as brave as you," she said in admiration.

"It is not bravery, Pinmei," Lady Meng said, reaching up to touch her cheek. "For I am not afraid. With my husband's death, I have nothing left to fear. You are the bravest of all of us, truly."

Lady Meng grasped both of their hands in hers. "Good journey, my young friends," she said. "If one of the greatest joys is encountering a friend far from home, making a friend must be as well.

"Now go," Lady Meng said, giving BaiMa a slap. The horse reared up, and Pinmei clung to Yishan, her braid whipping into the air. Then BaiMa leaped over the frozen waves onto the silver sea of ice.

CHAPTER
48

"There it is," Yishan said, pointing to the rolling mussel. It was quite a distance ahead of them, but they were still able to see it in the vast expanse of stillness and ice. But Yishan's direction was not needed, for BaiMa was already galloping toward the moving speck. Pinmei marveled at how he did not slip; his hooves burned into the waves of ice, and he ran as easily as if he were on a dirt road.

As BaiMa ran, the ice began to darken in color, white to gray, gray to dark gray, and when Pinmei raised her head, she saw a strange land before them—a rippling black surface dotted with feathery white flowers. But then the rolling mussel hopped into the air and splashed into the blackness. The bitter wind flew into Pinmei's open mouth. The black ground was water! The white flowers were pieces of frost! The ice was thinning!

Crack! The ice shattered under BaiMa's hooves, and Pinmei gasped as freezing water sprayed her, its coldness more startling than a slap. BaiMa reared, jumped onto thicker ice, and continued running.

"Are we going…" Pinmei panted. "Are we going to go…?"

Her words were lost in the wind, but Yishan turned his head to her. "Look at BaiMa!" he said.

Pinmei looked. Was BaiMa melting? Where the water had splashed him, his coat was washing away, leaving… scales? *Crack!* BaiMa's hooves broke through the ice again, and a large wave of water splashed over them. Again, Pinmei struggled to catch her breath, and this time the shock of the water felt as if her whole body had been struck.

But when she was finally able to think again, she gave an even greater gasp. For the water that had swept over BaiMa had washed away all his hair. His entire body was covered with luminous scales, and two horns had sprouted from his head. BaiMa opened his mouth and, instead of nickering, gave a loud roar that echoed across the ice.

"He's a *longma*!" Pinmei yelled so she could be heard above the sounds of the wind and the clopping hooves. "BaiMa's a dragon horse!"

Yishan nodded but instead of saying anything, he cocked his head forward. Pinmei gaped. The dark water was right in front of them, like the yawning mouth of a monster.

"We're going in," Yishan yelled back. "Hold tight!"

His last words were unnecessary. Pinmei clung to Yishan as if already drowning, her eyes as large as moons. BaiMa gave another roar, one so thunderous that the ice cracked behind them. He made a great leap, the force of the wind making Pinmei swallow her scream, and they all plunged into the blackness of the water.

CHAPTER
49

"Stonecutter!" the guard grunted. He let a bag drop to the floor, and it hit with the ringing sound of an iron bell. "These are for you!"

"Are they..." the stonecutter said, peering at the black bricks at the guard's feet, "stones?"

A second guard stomped in. He was older, and judging by the hostile glare he gave the prisoners, more brutish. "An old woman and a skeleton," he said, looking at them as if they were rice maggots. "They should just be executed and save us the trouble."

The stonecutter shrugged at Amah. Apparently, not all the soldiers valued her as the Storyteller.

The guard took a scroll of paper from his waistband and tossed it to the stonecutter.

"Those are the emperor's great deeds," he said as the stonecutter crawled on his hands and knees to retrieve the scroll. "Each must be carved in stone."

"The emperor's great deeds?" the stonecutter said. His eyes widened. "There are thousands!"

"We will bring you more stones when these are finished," the first guard said. He gave the stonecutter a packet that, when opened, contained stonecutting tools, and set down his lantern. Without another word, the guards marched away. The dungeon door clanked shut, leaving the prisoners staring at the pile of uncut stones in the flickering light.

"I suppose this is the use the Tiger King had in mind for me," the stonecutter said. "Why do you think he wishes this?"

"The emperor is not known for his humility," Amah said, "and great deeds carved in stone do have much power."

"Do they?" the stonecutter said, his eyes twinkling at Amah. "And is there a story about it?"

Amah had to smile at the stonecutter's impish grin. "There is," Amah said, "and I suppose I can tell it to you."

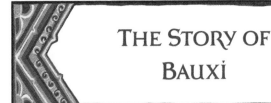

THE STORY OF BAUXI

My father told me that when his grandfather was a boy, it was not impossible for one to see a dragon or even a *longma*. While it would still be considered an extraordinary sight, people could believe it possible—unlike now, when most would think you were a liar or crazy.

For those were the days when beasts of the heavens and seas were still allowed to be seen by mortal eyes. That changed when the first king of the City of Bright Moonlight stopped the floods of his city.

Stopping the floods of the city seemed an impossible task. The first king realized that, instead of building dams, he must build waterways to redirect the river. But the work this required was enormous.

"I will supervise the men," the king's father said. "You have other things you must attend to."

With misgivings, the king allowed his father to oversee the project, for it was true that he had many other things to do. However, his misgivings proved correct, because his father was callous and cruel to the workers, forcing them to labor under harsh conditions from morning to night. When the king heard of this, he ordered his father to treat the workers better, but his father only argued.

"Do you want to stop the floods?" his father retorted. "We won't finish if the men are not worked so!"

The king saw his father was right, but he could not bear the sufferings of his people. Luckily, the Old Man of the Moon took pity on the young king and went to the Jade Emperor in the heavens and the Dragon King of the Sea on his behalf. Because of the Old Man's appeals, the dragon HuangLong was sent from the sky and the tortoise Bauxi (a distant cousin to the Black Tortoise of Winter) was sent from the sea to help the king.

Both creatures swore to stay on earth until the project was complete. And they were both much needed. The tortoise, with his incredible strength, would hold back the water while the dragon dredged the land. They worked tirelessly alongside the men, and the honor they brought to the city was relished by all, especially the king's father.

"The tortoise and the dragon are now my servants," the king's father said to him. "What will they do when the irrigation is complete?"

"They will leave," the king said.

"You must not let them!" the king's father said. "With them I am very powerful! I can even rival the power of the emperor himself!"

"They vowed to stay until the project is finished," the king said. "I cannot make them stay longer."

Then he left, missing the gleam in his father's eyes.

Over nine years later, the irrigation was completed. It was a grand success! The river flowed out to the land, gentle and docile, and the great floods were eased. But before the beasts could sit to rest, the king's father approached them.

"There is one last part of the project I need your help with," he said.

"Of course," the unsuspecting beasts replied.

"There is a grand monument I had made," the father said, leading them to a massive stone placard. It was as tall as a pine tree and covered with carved words. "I would like to have it carried to the river."

The placard was too heavy to lift, so the men had to dig a hole and lower it onto the tortoise's back. The good-natured tortoise shuffled into the pit, taking for granted that his immense strength could carry it out. However, as soon as the tablet was laid on his back,

Bauxi felt himself weighed deeper and deeper into the ground. He could not move! He was trapped.

"What have you done?" HuangLong said, looking at the king's father with suspicious eyes.

"That plaque lists all the great accomplishments of the world," the father said, a poorly hidden look of gloating in his eyes, "so of course you cannot carry it! And if you cannot carry it to the river, then the project is not complete and you both must stay here on earth!"

Bauxi sputtered and spat, but he was helpless. In frustration, he gave a great yowl, a protesting noise so full of resentment and anger the river water leaped in surprise. With a shudder, he turned into stone!

HuangLong turned to the king's father. "Bauxi has kept the oath," he said. "He will now never leave earth."

"And you?" the king's father asked.

"I too will keep the oath," HuangLong said. "But you will never benefit from it. From here on, I shall be invisible, and no mortal shall ever see me again."

And without another word, the dragon disappeared. The king's father looked around, aghast, but only the lifeless stone Bauxi, held down by the monument as if pinned by a needle, remained.

"Ah," the stonecutter said. "Tricking the beasts of heaven and sea! The king's father was crafty."

"Yes," Amah said. "But his trickery caused a great loss to all. For when the Jade Emperor heard what had happened, he was quite angry. He decreed that all beasts of the heavens would therefore no longer be seen by mortals."

"Which is why we do not see them today," the stonecutter said. He fingered the stones. "But why have me carve these? They are not stones for a monument. This is very common stone, to be placed someplace humble— like a country road or a wall."

"A wall?" Amah said, sitting up abruptly. She stared at the hill of stones, studying them.

"Ha!" the stonecutter said with a snort. "I suppose an entire wall of great accomplishments would be a fine cage for another poor tortoise!"

"Yes," Amah said, her eyes still on the stones. "It would."

CHAPTER
50

Pinmei was afraid to open her eyes. The shock of the cold water had been overwhelming, and she wasn't sure how long she had been lost in blackness. But now she felt strangely warm, as warm as if she had been dipped in a bath. The fabric of Yishan's shirt was still clenched in her fingers, and she swayed with the gentle motion of BaiMa's walking. Slowly, she opened her eyes.

Pinmei could not believe what she saw. It was early dusk, the deepening sky just beginning to fill with twinkling stars. BaiMa, still a dragon horse, his mane and mustache floating like the tentacles of a squid, walked on a road of white sand. The dark mussel was still rolling before them. The sand also twinkled in the light of the glowing lanterns that hung from red trees that lined the road. Red trees? Pinmei rubbed her eyes. They weren't trees! They were corals! And the glowing lanterns were jellyfish! She looked above again at the sky. The twinkling stars were really tiny swimming fish!

"Are we..." Pinmei gulped. "Are we at Sea Bottom?"

"Good, you're awake," Yishan said. "We're almost there."

Yishan motioned with his hand. In front of them was a field of waving sea grasses dotted with chrysanthemum flower anemones, but beyond that there was a silver glow in the darkening sky, as if the moon were rising.

"We're almost where?" Pinmei said.

"The Crystal Palace, silly!" said Yishan. In their descent, her braid had been flung over his shoulder; he now pulled it with a teasing tug. "Where else?"

As they got closer, the enormous, grand palace seemed to rise like a growing mountain. First they saw the roofs of crystal tile that glinted like the sun on rippling water. Then came the iridescent beams, carved and inlaid with gold and coral. After that were the translucent columns,

so lustrous Pinmei could see their gleam from the distance. All of it glowed with an ethereal light, and the sight made Pinmei catch her breath. How many stories had Amah told her about this place?

The sand road now changed to crystal brick, and BaiMa's hooves made the sound of tinkling bells. They passed white posts carved with grinning dragon faces and followed the mussel toward a long, raised walkway.

The mussel kept rolling forward. Pinmei found it comforting to watch. It was, perhaps, the only thing in the landscape she could truly believe. They passed shining pavilions, pearl-studded doors, and gates with purple-marbled arches. But the plain, humble shell continued to roll, oblivious to the splendor around it.

Even when it reached the grand staircase to the palace, the mussel continued, undaunted. Stone sculptures of sea creatures were stationed all around the bottom of the staircase to the gate of the great hall. As the mussel hopped up each step, Pinmei couldn't help looking away from their fierce stares. Even after they had passed, Pinmei suspected the stone figures turned their heads to continue their suspicious gazing.

But at the top of the steps, in the open archway of the palace entrance, the mussel stopped.

"I guess we're officially here," Yishan said, slipping off the horse and walking toward the door. Pinmei followed, but then BaiMa gave a low, triumphant bellow.

They turned to look at the dragon horse. He walked over to the edge of the entrance platform and, without warning, he leaped over the guard posts.

Yishan and Pinmei raced to the edge of the landing. Below, BaiMa was circling an empty platform next to one of the stone statues. With a graceful leap, he jumped onto it and gave another roar, one of great joy and satisfaction. As if settling in for a well-deserved rest, he folded his scaly legs and sat. A solid stillness covered him, and Pinmei saw his legs meld into the stone platform. BaiMa had turned into a statue.

Pinmei stared, openmouthed. "Do you think Lady Meng knew?" she whispered.

Yishan shrugged, his cocked head making him seem more curious than awed. But before he could say anything, another voice sounded behind them!

"So you're back, are you?" the voice said. "Have a good trip?"

CHAPTER
51

Pinmei and Yishan spun around. In the arched entrance-way, a figure robed in silver-gray was kneeling and speaking to the mussel.

"No, your parents didn't miss you," he was saying to the mussel. "They're still in their winter sleep, right in their mussel shells, like all the other swallows... Yes, when everyone wakes up in the spring, I'll tell them you aren't making it up, it was not just a dream..."

The man looked up and saw the children. He smiled. It was a broad grin, almost as if he had just told them a secret joke. It was so open and warm that Pinmei smiled back.

"Hello!" he said, standing up. As he did, Pinmei saw that he leaned heavily on a coral cane and one of his pant legs hung empty. The hand that clutched the cane had a long, deep scar that went up his arm under his sleeve. His face also had a long scar across it, but his eyes sparkled with such merriment that it was barely noticeable. He rushed over to them eagerly.

"Ah, you've come!" he said, grasping their hands with the affection of a long-lost friend. "The Sea King has been quite impatient for you, especially after yesterday. He thought you were being abominably slow, but of course, time is so different up there. A long time for us is a short time for you, or is it the other way around? I think it goes back and forth—like waves of the sea, you know."

"Do we know you?" Pinmei asked. The man's disarming manner was so forthcoming she couldn't help wondering if he had mistaken them for others.

"Maybe!" the man said, laughing. It was such a joyful noise that it seemed to tickle. Pinmei and Yishan couldn't help laughing too, though Pinmei wasn't sure what was so funny. "I've been called many names up there. Stone Fish, Happy Fish, Not a Dragon, Special Treasure, Gift...Of course, my favorite one was Joy to the Heart. Such a nice girl gave it to me. What was her name...Meizi? Meiyi? No, it was Meiya..."

"Joy to the Heart?" Pinmei repeated, feeling her thoughts beginning to swim.

"I know it's a bit of a mouthful, but—" the man started.

"I do know you!" Pinmei interrupted. "You're in the stories! You are the fish that was given to the first king of the City of Bright Moonlight!"

"Ah! I am remembered!" the man said, pleased. "It's been a while since I've been up top. I was sure I'd be forgotten by now. Fame is so fleeting, you know."

"But, you're not a fish anymore?" Pinmei asked. "You're a man now?"

"Oh," he said. "We only take on these forms in honor of the Sea King. He used to be a mortal man, so he's most comfortable like that. So since he's most often in human form, all who live at Sea Bottom do the same while we're here."

Pinmei scarcely heard him. "If you were the stone fish," she said, still thinking hard, "that means you were also the statue for the magistrate that broke..."

"Yes," Joy to the Heart said, making a face and lifting his cane. "That's when I lost part of my tail and cracked my fin. Not a big deal when I'm in fish form, but it's a bit inconvenient here at Sea Bottom."

"Couldn't you just be half fish or something?" Yishan asked. "You could just have a fish tail."

"Oh no!" Joy to the Heart said, looking shocked. "I would never dream of that! For me to have a fish tail in this form would be an insult to the fish-tail goddess, Nuwa! The only one who is allowed to take on a form like that is the princess."

"Why?" Yishan asked.

"Because she was born that way," Joy to the Heart said with pride. "It was a great blessing to His Majesty! His child born in Nuwa's likeness! That was an occasion, I can tell you!"

"It's because the Sea King swallowed the red stone," Pinmei said, her thoughts now leaping and diving. "The red stone was Nuwa's last drop of blood. Some of Nuwa's blood must be in the princess, which is why she has a fish tail."

Joy to the Heart wasn't listening. Instead he was leaning against the terrace railing. "What a celebration that was!" he said, lost in the memory. "They painted the whole sky with colored water. A picture would form and melt away into another! And what pictures! Pictures of the king shaping the tear into a pearl, of Nuwa fixing the sky!" he said, stretching out his arm. "And, of course, of the princess." His smile waned slightly as he placed his hand on the railing. "Poor princess," he said softly. "I hope she's doing well."

"Why?" Yishan asked. "Why wouldn't she be?"

"She left some time ago... When was it...?" Joy to the Heart said. "The last time I saw her was when I gave her that needle from the treasury... What's that?"

"What?" Pinmei and Yishan said in unison, looking around. Joy to the Heart raised his cane and pointed at BaiMa.

"There's a new *longma*!" he said with excitement, and then with even more excitement said, "Why, it's BaiMa! He finally got his immortal form!"

"You know him?" Pinmei asked, surprised.

"Well, I knew him as a stone," Joy to the Heart said. "He was like me, a stone that dreams of becoming something else. Here at Sea Bottom, we can look almost any way we want, but to actually become something else forever, we need the help of someone up there."

"Why?" Pinmei asked.

"Why?" Joy to the Heart looked puzzled, as if he had never thought about it before. "I don't know. Mortals are the only ones who can give immortality. It has always been that way."

"What do you mean?" Pinmei asked. His words made her thoughts twist and snarl as if they were a tangle of seaweed.

Joy to the Heart looked even more perplexed, his smile transforming into a frown. "Well, I guess it's because it's the mortals who create the memories that last," he said, scratching his head. "Without those, immortals forget. They can even forget who they are. Right?"

He looked at Yishan, who only shrugged back at him. "There's a lot of stuff I don't remember, but I know who I am," Yishan said. He grinned. "How about you, Pinmei?"

She made a face at him while Joy to the Heart frowned again in confusion. Finally, he shook his head. "Anyway, how do you know BaiMa?"

"Actually," Yishan said, "we rode him here."

"Did you now?" Joy to the Heart said, his smile returning. "Well, why not? Shall we go?"

"Where?" said Pinmei.

"To see the Sea King, of course! Isn't that why you are here?" Joy to the Heart said, laughing, "Come along. I'm sure he's waiting."

CHAPTER
52

Pinmei and Yishan followed Joy to the Heart through the crystal-paved entranceway and the courtyard to the palace's great hall. At the doorway, two guards stood. The guards were so similar in appearance Pinmei had to check and make sure one was not just a reflection. Both of them had beady eyes and long, thin whiskers that sprouted from their noses and chins.

"Hello, my laughing fellows!" Joy to the Heart said cheerfully. The two guards did not smile back. "Some guests to see His Majesty! They're from up there!"

Joy to the Heart pointed his cane upward, narrowly missing one of the guard's feather helmets.

"Hey, watch it!" the guard said. After making sure his helmet was straight, he asked, "It's been tense around here since yesterday's visitor. Is one of these the one he called for?"

"Must be," Joy to the Heart said, winking at the children. "They rode in on a *longma*."

"They are kind of small," the other guard said. "Aren't they usually bigger?"

"Come, now," Joy to the Heart said in answer. "You of all creatures should know how little size matters."

Pinmei caught Yishan's grin. "They're really shrimp," he mouthed to her.

"Good point," the other guard said, and he pushed open the door. "Come along."

When they entered, Pinmei felt as if they had stepped inside a pearl. Everything was illuminated with a soft white light. Beautiful women and men glided around the room, their flowing robes waving a dance of color as they moved.

"Visitors from above!" the guard hollered.

All went silent and Pinmei knew what a fish in a bowl felt like, for hundreds of large eyes stared at her. She flinched, but one pair of eyes fixed a gaze so piercing upon her that she could not look away. They were, of course, the eyes of the Sea King.

A thin silver mist emanated from him, and his beard fell like a cascading waterfall. The deep ridge of his forehead was finished with two branched dragon horns, one on each side of his head, and the broad nostrils of his nose flared. As he stood, his robes shimmered, the purple shifting until it was the same deep blue of his jasper scepter.

"Come!" he roared.

The shrimp guard pushed them forward. Pinmei stumbled, pulling Yishan with her so they both ended up in the humblest of kowtows. The king sat back slowly in his water-jade throne, his eyes still fastened on them as his jaw stiffened with displeasure. He motioned for them to rise, allowing Yishan to fix his hat before addressing him.

"You are children!" the Sea King said, the frown on his face darkening. "You cannot be . . ."

"I am Yishan." He motioned to Pinmei. "And this is the Storyteller's granddaughter."

"Pinmei," she said, lifting her head. Her voice thinned in the air as she flushed. "I'm Pinmei."

"Yes," Yishan said, a smile teasing his mouth. "Pinmei is the Storyteller's granddaughter." His shoulders lifted and his face straightened. "What did you call for?"

Pinmei sneaked a glance at Yishan. He was staring intently at the Sea King, who was looking back at him, the brow above his blank eyes creased in a cavernous fold. Perhaps Yishan thought it best just to act as if he understood what the Sea King was talking about. Pinmei pressed her lips together.

Finally, the Sea King snorted. He lifted his fingers at the guard. "Bring yesterday's visitor," he ordered.

As the guard clattered away, the Sea King turned to them.

"I called about the winter," the king said. "The upper waters are starting to freeze."

"We know," Yishan said.

"When I realized even my royal powers could only unfreeze the water for a moment," the king continued, raising an eyebrow, "I knew I had to alert those above, which is why I lit the beacons."

The Sea King stopped and looked at them dubiously.

"Yes?" Yishan said, and Pinmei was surprised at his tone of impatience.

"The breath of the Black Tortoise is overpowering everything," the king said. "He has been here too long."

"It is not for us to dictate his stay," Yishan said. "He has his mandate."

Pinmei felt her mouth falling open as she stared at Yishan. He could not just be pretending. Yishan seemed to be standing taller, his face unusually serious and authoritative. What had happened to him? And what was he talking about?

"I know!" the Sea King said, annoyed. "But this is different! The Black Tortoise is in trouble!"

"The Black Tortoise is invincible," Yishan scoffed. "What could harm him?"

"I don't know," the Sea King said. "But he needs help."

"The Black Tortoise needs help?" Yishan said, and it was his voice that was full of doubt this time. "How do you know that?"

As if in response, there was a clatter of the guard returning.

"Here!" the guard bellowed.

The group of watching nobles, their robes swaying, parted to make a path. All were silent, and Pinmei squinted, for she could not see what person they were shifting for.

But then she saw. It was not a person at all. Instead, slithering toward them like a twisting piece of black string, was a snake.

CHAPTER
53

"Come," the Sea King said to the snake, waving his hand. "Tell these children what you told me."

The black snake slunk forward, and Pinmei saw it slide through the air, only an inch or so above the floor. The snake turned and looked at them with tiny eyes like knotted black threads.

"The Black Tortoise needs help," hissed the snake, its voice like the wind through pine needles.

"What kind of help?" Yishan asked. "What has happened to him?"

The snake turned back to the Sea King, stretching its

neck as if pleading. "The Black Tortoise needs help," it hissed again.

"Yes, but..." Yishan began.

"It says nothing else," the Sea King interrupted. The snake moved to coil itself next to the Sea King's throne. "I do not think it can. But you see, do you not? The Black Tortoise is in trouble."

Yishan nodded. Pinmei raised her eyebrows at him to try to get his attention, but he continued to look directly at the Sea King.

"You are right when you said nothing could harm the Black Tortoise," the Sea King said. "But something must be keeping him from leaving. I know little of your world these days, but I do know it is in your world that the tortoise is trapped. You"—the Sea King hesitated, obviously skeptical—"or someone up there must free him."

Yishan nodded, and Pinmei finally felt she could not let him continue. What was he doing? Why was Yishan talking to the Sea King about the Black Tortoise and winter? Were they even going to ask about the stone? With a surreptitious glance at the king, she jabbed Yishan sharply with her elbow.

He yelped and looked guiltily at her glare.

"Actually, we're here for another reason too," Pinmei

said, hoping her voice did not squeak as much as it did in her ears. "We'd like to ask about a Luminous Stone That Lights the Night."

"A Luminous Stone That Lights the Night?" the Sea King said in surprise. "It has been a long time since I have heard Nuwa's tear called that."

"Nuwa's tear?" Pinmei said, frowning.

"Yes," the Sea King said. "When Nuwa, the great goddess with the fish tail, sacrificed herself to save the sky, the earth, and the seas, she left behind three things. Do you remember what they are, Storyteller's granddaughter?"

Pinmei looked up at the Sea King, but his eyes were as unreadable as black waves of water. She nodded.

"Her husband pulled out a strand of hair as Nuwa transformed," Pinmei said.

"The Iron Rod," the Sea King said.

"When he pulled the hair, there was a drop of blood," Pinmei continued.

"The Red Stone," the king said, and he touched his chest.

"But, before that," Pinmei said slowly, "Nuwa shed a single tear in sorrow."

"A Luminous Stone That Lights the Night," the Sea King finished. He drew himself up proudly. "I am honored to have all three of these items in my dominion."

"Y-you do?" Pinmei stuttered. "You have the Luminous Stone?"

"A stone rests in my kingdom," the Sea King said. "At least, partly."

"Can we see it?" Pinmei asked. All her irritation and confusion disappeared in her eagerness. The Luminous Stone was here! They were so close! "Please!"

"That is easy enough," the Sea King said, and without warning he stood up. All the attendants and nobles sprang up in a flurry, rippling out like waves in the water. "Come," he said. "Let us go see the Luminous Stone That Lights the Night."

CHAPTER

54

The Sea King waved away his servants and attendants with a flick of his hand and motioned for the children to follow. The black snake silently uncoiled itself and slithered alongside.

"Yishan," Pinmei whispered fiercely, pulling him to fall behind the king's billowing robes. "What was that about?"

"What?" Yishan said with pretended innocence.

Pinmei glared.

"It worked out, didn't it?" he said. "We're going to see the stone right now."

She looked at him with narrowed eyes as he grinned at her.

"Hey," Yishan called as the Sea King led them out of the palace. "Aren't we going to the treasury?"

The Sea King turned and looked at Yishan with his eyebrow raised, the disbelieving look returning to his face.

"To see Nuwa's Tear," the Sea King said, "we must go to the garden. Do you not know that?"

"Oh, um, yes," Yishan said quickly. He reddened as if truly embarrassed. "I just forgot."

"Hmm," the Sea King said, his nostrils flaring. He continued to walk. "The garden is this way."

It was not like any garden Pinmei had ever seen before, not even in her dreams. Again, jellyfish lanterns lit their way, making the crystal stones of the mosaic pathway sparkle. There were flowers of unimaginable colors, their closed blossoms like polished shells. Heavy with glossy pink and white fruits, the coral tree branches swayed softly above her. No, not fruits, Pinmei realized, shaking her head. *Pearls!*

They reached a bridge and, with a hiss, the snake slithered away. Almost soundlessly, it splashed into the water and vanished. Pinmei could not even see a faint shadow of it as they began to walk over the lake . . . or was it an ocean? The bridge stretched and stretched only to disappear, and Pinmei could not even imagine where it ended.

"Are we walking over the sea?" Pinmei asked faintly.

"This is the Heavenly Lake," the Sea King told her. "The immortals of the sky call it the Celestial River and you mortals call it the Starry River, but here we call it the Heavenly Lake. I suppose to us at Sea Bottom, it seems more the size of a lake than a river."

"But the Starry River is the sky," Pinmei said, shaking her head in confusion. "It's up high. This is below!"

The Sea King nodded. "Our worlds connect here," he said. "The bottom of the Heavenly Lake is your sky."

Pinmei could only stare. The water below them was as smooth as a jade plate and melted into the horizon. It was as if she were walking through an infinite night sky, and it was making her dizzy. After another long pause, the Sea King stopped and brought them to the edge of the bridge.

"Here it is," he said, and waved his hands toward the water below. A soft glow shone from the reflections on the lake, bathing them all in light. "Nuwa's tear," he said with reverence, "or a Luminous Stone That Lights the Night."

Or, Pinmei thought as she stared downward, *the moon*.

CHAPTER
55

Both Yishan and Pinmei gazed down at the moon. It was a perfect, glowing circle in the still black water, and the reflection of the thousands of fish above twinkled around it exactly like stars. Pinmei felt as if she were looking down at the night sky.

"It's beautiful, is it not?" the Sea King said. "A Luminous Stone That Lights the Night," the Sea King finished, motioning downward. "I myself found it long, long ago. I shaped it into a dragon's pearl, but it was never meant to belong to one being. It belongs to everyone in the sea, sky, and earth. That is why it floats in the Heavenly Lake, so all can see it."

"Of course," Yishan whispered, almost angrily. "I am such a fool. Why didn't I remember...? I should've realized..."

"How would you?" Pinmei said. "Who would have thought the moon would be at the bottom of the sea?" The pure light stroked her face with the tenderness of a mother, and she felt a wave of anguish. The moon! They were here to take it to the emperor. But how could they?

"Why did you wish to see it?" the Sea King asked.

"We need to take it," Yishan said. "To give to the emperor."

"What?" the Sea King said, and began to laugh, a deep, roaring laugh. His head arched back and his hand thumped against his chest in amusement. "You! Take Nuwa's tear? That is the most ridiculous thing I have ever heard!"

"It's not ridiculous!" Yishan flashed, his face the color of his hat.

"A little goldfish like you?" The Sea King laughed again. "You are a fool! You could not even lift it from the lake, much less carry it from the sea!"

"I can!" Yishan was shouting like a spoiled child, and

he moved as if to climb over the railing to dive into the water.

"Yishan!" Pinmei hissed, grabbing him. "Stop it! What is wrong with you?"

"He's laughing at me!" Yishan huffed. "He called me a fool!"

"Well, if you dive into that lake to try to get the moon, you are!" Pinmei said. "The lake is the sky! You could be falling forever!"

Yishan grabbed Pinmei's wrists to push her away, but his fingers caught on her string bracelet. Suddenly, he stopped struggling.

"You're right," he said. The resentment disappeared from his face and was replaced by a mischievous expression that puzzled Pinmei even more than his anger.

"Anyway, I don't need to jump into the lake," he said. He gave the Sea King a smug look. "I can get the moon another way."

CHAPTER
56

"Y-you can?" Pinmei stuttered, confused.

Yishan grinned, and Pinmei felt hope bubble inside her. Maybe he could! And if he could, they could still save Amah!

"Just let me borrow back that bracelet," Yishan said to her.

She gave Yishan a baffled look, but rolled the string off her wrist and handed it to him. He gently tugged at the knot until one end of the string was pulled out, forming a small lasso.

"There!" he said, and began to move to the edge of the bridge.

"Yishan, you're just teasing!" Pinmei groaned. "You know that's much too small! It'll never reach the water, and it won't fit around the moon either!"

"You'll see," Yishan said, giving her braid a tug.

He bent over the bridge rail and dangled the lasso from his hand. Together, the Sea King and Pinmei leaned over to watch. They both gasped in disbelief.

The small circle continued to lower, going down, down toward the water, and the string in Yishan's hand stretched longer and longer.

Noiselessly, the ring slid into the lake. Was the water magnifying it, or was the loop getting bigger? When it finally wavered next to the moon, it looked as if it were the moon's empty outline.

Pinmei stole a glance at Yishan. Had he somehow gained a magic power? But Yishan still looked like the same boy, tilted dangerously over the bridge's railing, now with the tip of his tongue sticking out from the corner of his mouth. "Almost there," he whispered.

He flicked his wrist and the string circle swayed, missing the moon entirely. Yishan grumbled, twitched his wrist, and missed again. He did this over and over again until—

"Ha!" Yishan said. Finally, on his sixth try, the loop neatly encircled the shining moon. Yishan grunted with satisfaction and began to pull, the noose tightening around the moon until the delicate thread looked like a thin scratch of blood.

Slowly, carefully, Yishan began to lift the moon. It grew larger and larger until the great globe seemed to be filling the lake. And as it came closer, its glow became stronger and brighter, with a brilliance so dazzling Pinmei could scarcely bear to look at it. The light was whiter than snow, whiter than ice, whiter than the purest flower or pearl. The black waters and sky turned a shimmering silver, and Pinmei felt as if she could drink its radiance.

"You...are...thieves!" A choked noise broke the spell of their awe. Pinmei and Yishan looked away from the moon to see the Sea King, and both froze.

His mouth was gaping and his arms were reaching out helplessly toward the luminous water. But it was his eyes that made them stop. Those eyes, which had been so unreadable before, were now illuminated with the light of the moon, and they were filled with horror and revulsion.

"You would steal..." the king continued, his words strangled noises. "It does not belong to you...not to only one...How...how could you?"

Yishan saw the disgusted eyes of the young boy that the Sea King had been, the great hero who had refused to hurt anyone, even to save himself. Pinmei saw the eyes of Amah, dismayed and disappointed.

Suddenly, they were both ashamed. Pinmei and Yishan looked at each other, stricken.

"Put it back," Pinmei ordered. "Put the moon back. We can't trade Amah for the moon. We...the emperor... have no right to take it."

Yishan nodded. He lowered the string, and the glorious brightness began to dim. The enormous ball got smaller and smaller until, finally, it was only a glowing circle on the black silk of the night. Yishan shook his wrist to remove the string, and all watched as the released moon returned to its place in the limitless Heavenly Lake. Yishan breathed a sigh of relief.

"I don't think the emperor's going to get his Luminous Stone," he said.

CHAPTER
57

Pinmei smiled feebly at Yishan, but when their eyes met, she knew they were both aghast at what they had almost done. Yishan looked over at the Sea King. Even now, the Sea King was leaning motionlessly over the bridge, the glow of the moon on his still-concerned face.

"Don't worry! We're not going to take it," Yishan called out. The Sea King raised his head to look at him. "We were just, uh, joking," Yishan finished lamely.

To Pinmei's surprise, the Sea King turned to them and bowed to Yishan. "I apologize. I should not have doubted you," he said with a respect one gives to an equal. "I should have realized that even while young, you could still..."

"It's nothing," Yishan said, cutting him off. His face flushed again, this time from shame.

Pinmei's hands were trembling, and she felt her knees quake. Weakly, she sat down, her back against the carved stone wall of the bridge. Her hand rubbed her wrist, naked without Amah's bracelet or even the red string. Yishan, waving away any further words from the Sea King, sat next to her.

"I got carried away," Yishan admitted in a low tone. "But the moon isn't something the emperor should have. We can't take it."

"Amah wouldn't want us to anyway," Pinmei said. Just thinking of Amah cut into her chest, but she knew her words were true. Amah would never want them to take the moon out of the sky. She would be horrified by the thought. But without the Luminous Stone, without the moon, would she ever see Amah again? The blackness of the sea suddenly overwhelmed her; it was nothing more than a vast emptiness. Pinmei's eyes stung with tears.

"You're right," Yishan said after a long moment. He handed her the damp string bracelet, returned to its original size. "We'll find another way to get Amah back."

Pinmei nodded and rolled the bracelet onto her wrist, not meeting his eyes. Despite Yishan's assured tone, she knew it was a hollow hope. There was no other way. What else could they do?

Tears continued to fill her eyes, and she reached into her sleeve for her handkerchief. But, as Pinmei brought it to her face, she realized she was holding the Paper of Answers. She stared at it, and shafts of light from the full moon below streamed in through carved openings behind her.

"If there is another way to get Amah," Pinmei said, waving the clutched paper at Yishan, "this is how we can find out!"

CHAPTER
58

"What?" Yishan said, startled and confused.

"The Paper will answer any question in the light of the full moon," Pinmei said, waving the Paper toward the dark water. "The moon is full here! And any immortal can read the Paper—the emperor said so, remember?"

"An immortal?" Yishan asked.

Pinmei cocked her head over at the Sea King.

"You mean, ask him to read it for us?" Yishan said.

Pinmei rolled her eyes. "Yes!" she said. "The Paper can tell us if there is another way to get Amah!"

Yishan took the Paper from Pinmei, his hands caressing it in an almost loving gesture. Then he stood.

"Your Majesty," he said as Pinmei scrambled to her feet, "we have a favor to ask you."

The Sea King stepped forward. "Ah, just a paper now?" he asked. "Not a book anymore?"

Pinmei's words rushed out in her eagerness. "It's the Paper of Answers," she said. "If we ask it a question, can you read us the answer?"

"Yes," the Sea King said, but he had a puzzled look on his face. "But surely—"

"Thank you," Yishan said in a voice that made both Pinmei and the Sea King quiet. Yishan stepped closer to the edge of the bridge, holding the Paper in front of him as if offering it to the sky.

Pinmei tingled with such excitement that she felt she could have been one of the flickering fish above. They could still save Amah! The Paper knew everything!

Yishan was already speaking. In a loud voice, each word like a stone dropping into water, he asked his question.

"How has the emperor captured the Black Tortoise of Winter?" Yishan said.

CHAPTER
59

Pinmei shrieked a sound of disbelief.

"Yishan!" she hissed. "What about Amah? You were supposed to ask about Amah!"

Yishan said nothing and just looked at her sheepishly, holding the Paper away from her as she flew at him. Dark marks were already forming on the page.

"Why did you ask about the tortoise?" Pinmei said, unable to stop. "How will we ever get Amah now?"

Her last words ripped out of her in a wail, plaintive and piercing. But the cry, so raw in her throat, disappeared in the blackness like a single tear falling into the sea.

"Pinmei," Yishan said in a wheedling tone, "we'll get her back."

"How?" Pinmei said accusingly.

"The emperor wants Amah for her stories, right?" Yishan said. "You know all the stories too. We can figure it out ourselves."

"Figure it out ourselves?" she said, glaring. "We wouldn't have to if you hadn't asked the Paper about... about... the tortoise!"

"Listen," Yishan said, coaxing her, "I had to ask about the tortoise. We need to save Amah from the emperor, right? Well, how do you think he suddenly became so powerful? He's captured the tortoise. That's why it's still winter and the emperor is invincible."

If one could make the Black Tortoise do anything, that person would be invincible, Amah had said. Could Yishan be right? If the emperor had the Black Tortoise of Winter, he was invincible, and they knew the emperor had taken Amah because he wanted to be immortal. Did the emperor plan on being invincible forever?

Pinmei looked at Yishan, and his eyes gazed into hers with a rare earnestness.

"It's not just Amah who needs to be rescued," Yishan said, and suddenly Pinmei thought of Lady Meng and the slave workers of the Vast Wall, the hollow eyes of the king of the City of Bright Moonlight, the tearstained faces of the village children, and Suya's emptying rice jar. Pinmei closed her eyes. The emperor. The tortoise. The winter. Amah. Was it somehow all sewn together? And was the Black Tortoise the stitch that needed to be pulled first before it could all unravel?

Pinmei opened her eyes, but she still saw Amah's face in her mind. Her chest felt as if the weight of the moon pressed against it, but she slowly nodded. "You're right," she said, the words dry in her mouth.

Yishan smiled gratefully. He turned to the Sea King, who had been watching them in uncomfortable silence.

"Please, Your Majesty," Yishan said, handing the Sea King the Paper, "could you read this?"

The king took the Paper with an uneasy look on his face, and he gave Yishan a questioning glance. But he held the Paper over his head. His eyes widened.

"What does it say?" Yishan asked. "How has the emperor captured the tortoise?"

"It says," the Sea King said as he lowered the Paper, the look of shock still on his face, "with the Iron Rod."

CHAPTER

60

"That makes sense," Yishan muttered, more to himself than to the others. "What else could hold the Black Tortoise? It's the only thing! The Iron Rod!"

"The Iron Rod?" Pinmei asked, the king's confused look now on her own face as well. "Isn't that...Nuwa's hair? Isn't that here..."

Instead of answering, the Sea King opened his mouth, and a roar, like the rushing of waves, sounded. Before the call could even echo, two figures appeared. They were obviously royal guards or generals, for their heavy copper-colored armor almost completely encased them, with only tufts of fur peeking out. As they bowed low, it was easy to imagine them as transformed crabs.

"Go to the treasury," the king said, "and see if the Iron Rod is there."

The two guards bowed again and, with a flash, disappeared.

The Sea King turned back to the children.

"If the Iron Rod has been stolen, it must be found immediately," he said to them gravely. "It is much too powerful to be misused, as I fear it has been already."

"The emperor must have gotten it," Yishan said.

"I do not understand how," the Sea King said. "We do not heavily guard it, for only an immortal could take it from Sea Bottom. Your emperor must have gotten an immortal to steal it for him."

"Or he just got lucky," Yishan said darkly. "The emperor has a bit of an obsession with immortality."

Pinmei looked at Yishan, a hundred questions silently filling her open mouth. He looked like the same boy she had always known, but he was acting as if he were as powerful as the Sea King. But before she could force out a word, a clicking sounded behind them. The two crab guards had returned.

"The Iron Rod is not in the treasury, Your Majesty," one of the guards said.

"You checked carefully?" the Sea King asked. "You know the Iron Rod can shrink to the size of a needle."

The guards nodded.

"Begin a search for it at once, then," the Sea King said. "Question all the servants and check all who have ever been to the Treasury. Make sure to ask the queen and her handmaids; sometimes they use it for their sewing and other fine work. If the Iron Rod is in the sea, I want it found."

The guards bobbed and bowed, and with more clicking, they disappeared again. The Sea King looked once more at the children.

"But I think we know the Iron Rod is unlikely to be found in the sea," he said to them. "So it looks as if the task of retrieving it will be up to you, my small friends."

"We'll go immediately," Yishan said.

"Do you not wish to rest after your travels?" the Sea King said courteously. "It would honor me to host—"

"That's not necessary," Yishan interrupted. "We've been away long enough, and with time being different down here and everything, who knows what has happened up there?"

"Very true," the Sea King said. He bowed respectfully and said, "I will take you to the surface."

"You will take us?" Pinmei coughed.

As if in reply, the Sea King straightened and let out another roar, this one long and thunderous. His robes billowed out in colossal waves, flowing past Pinmei and Yishan. The silk settled onto a massive, powerful shape and transformed into iridescent scales. When Pinmei finally dared to look back at the Sea King, she saw his head had elongated, with deep brows shadowing his glittering eyes and his horns now majestic. The Sea King had changed into a dragon.

"Come," he said, his voice sounding as if it were coming from the depths of the sea.

Yishan quickly clambered onto the dragon's back and held out his hand to Pinmei. "Hurry up."

Pinmei stared. The dragon's scales shimmered and glistened; he was a gigantic mountain of luminous colors and light. As she hesitated, the dragon turned his head toward her, his impenetrable black eyes piercing her.

"Come, Storyteller's granddaughter," he said. "You will be needed too."

Pinmei nodded and, without taking Yishan's hand, climbed onto the dragon's back.

CHAPTER
61

The stonecutter waited for Amah to awaken before he started work. He watched as her eyes opened, but to his dismay, he saw them fill with tears.

"It is nothing," Amah said, wiping her tears and waving him away. "I dreamed of my granddaughter, and when I woke to see the bars of the prison cell..."

"I know," the stonecutter said, reaching for her hand. Tears filled his eyes as well. "Sometimes I wonder if the face I remember is truly my daughter's."

"I hope they are both safe and protected," Amah said as another tear fell.

"My friend," the stonecutter said, "perhaps that is not a thing to hope for. You lived on the mountain because you wished your granddaughter to be safe. But even on the mountain, danger came. For, truly, the safest place in the world is this prison cell."

Amah stared at the stonecutter and slowly nodded. "You are wise," she said, "wiser than me."

"No," the stonecutter said, shaking his head. "I am just a common stonecutter."

"Hardly," Amah said as she looked with appreciation at his finely cut stones. "You are quite a master."

"Ah, this is nothing," the stonecutter said humbly, waving his hand. "If I only had my own tools or just a chisel of good quality...then perhaps I could make something worthy of you calling me that."

"It is your skill, not the tools, that make you master," Amah said. "Just like Painter Chen and his magic paintbrush. It needed the skill of a master."

"I do not know that story," the stonecutter said. "Tell me."

The Story of the Magic Paintbrush

There was once a boy named Liang who longed to be an artist. But as he was the son of a poor fisherman, there seemed little opportunity for him to become one. Nevertheless, he would draw whenever he could. Everyplace he went was covered with his drawings.

What Liang wished for most was a paintbrush. He would often sneak to the studio of the local craftsman and watch him make paintbrushes and inkstones, hoping there would be a discarded one for him to take. Unfortunately for him, there was never anything—not a swath of goat hair or even a piece of stone—for the boy to take.

But one day, Liang was alone on his father's boat in the water. He was supposed to be minding the fishing nets, but he had found a fine piece of bamboo and was using it to draw pictures with water on the inside of the boat. So, he was quite surprised when the boat pulled violently, the motion matched with a pained cry.

Liang looked over the edge of the boat, and there, under the surface of the water, was the figure of a girl. Her hair had gotten tangled in his fishnets and she was pulling to free herself with such force she was sure to drag his boat under. Quickly, the boy took out his knife and cut the girl's hair. Freed, the girl swiftly disappeared without even looking at him. But as she swam away, he saw that instead of legs, she had a fish tail.

Liang scratched his head, almost believing it had been a dream. But when he pulled up his fishnets, he saw the lock of hair was still caught in it. As he pulled out the strands of hair, he marveled at its texture. So smooth and delicate, they were almost like threads of water. The boy stared at it.

Using the twine from his fishnet, he quickly attached the hair to his bamboo stick.

"A fine brush!" Liang cried out in joy.

And it was indeed a fine brush. Liang did not realize how wonderful the brush was, however, until he dipped it into the water and painted a frog on the wood of his boat. To his amazement, when he finished, a real frog croaked from his picture and jumped away!

With such a brush, Liang's life changed. He painted ink and paper for himself, a magnificent boat for his father, and a luxurious silk robe for his mother. Everything he painted came to life, and all around him rejoiced.

The news of the magic paintbrush reached the ears of a new, young judge of the village. This judge was not only new, but was also unscrupulous. He quietly ordered some thugs to steal Liang's paintbrush.

When Liang's paintbrush was brought to the young judge, he eagerly began to paint. With the finest ink and paper, he painted a mountain of gold, but only a pile of dirty stones sprang from the page. He tried to paint a bowl of gold ingots, but instead a bowl of foul-smelling, rotten dumplings formed. Finally, he decided to paint a simple bar of gold. But when he finished, the bar turned into a vicious yellow snake and the judge had to call his servants to get rid of it.

Realizing he could not use the paintbrush himself, the judge had Liang brought to him.

"I heard your paintbrush was stolen," the judge said to him craftily, "so I had my officers search for it, and we've found it. I'm happy to return it to you."

Liang, of course, was suspicious, but he thanked the judge and reached to retrieve his special brush.

"Do you think," the judge said, again in a wily tone, holding the brush just out of Liang's reach, "you could paint something for me, before you go?"

Liang knew this was all a ploy, yet he could only nod.

"What do you wish a picture of?" Liang asked.

"It would be nice to have some gold," the judge said. "Perhaps a chest or two?"

"Ah, but a chest of gold would eventually empty," Liang said, thinking hard. "You need the Golden Chicken. It lays eggs of pure gold."

"A chicken that lays eggs of gold?" the judge said, his eyes lighting with greed. "Yes, that sounds perfect."

So, taking the brush, Liang painted a chicken with golden feathers and red eyes. The chicken clucked and immediately laid an egg of solid gold. The judge fell upon his knees to collect it.

"I'll go now," said Liang. The judge nodded, barely noticing the boy's departure as he crawled behind the chicken to catch more eggs.

Many weeks later, the judge had collected a room full of golden eggs—the door to the room was locked with a special key only he carried. The chicken was given a special henhouse surrounded by a high, secure fence. But one day, as the chicken was pecking bugs outside, a soft rain fell. Immediately, the chicken disappeared, and in its place was a wet piece of paper, a blurry painting of a chicken on it.

The judge, after the fury of losing the chicken subsided, comforted himself with his roomful of golden eggs. But soon after, a terrible smell came from the judge's residence. The servants finally traced it to the judge's locked room. When he opened the door, all almost fainted from the foul odor. The room was full of rotten eggs.

Even more enraged, the judge called for Liang to be brought to him. But Liang had left the village long ago. On the day he had painted the chicken, he had hurried home, said goodbye, and, after painting a giant crane, jumped on its back, and flown away.

Liang changed his name to Chen, hid his brush, and found a great master artist to study under. When he grew to manhood, he finally took out his magic brush again. But he made sure he never finished any of his paintings so they would not come to life. His horses' eyes were never dotted, his fish's scales were incomplete, and his figures were missing a shoe. However, even with these flaws, his artistry became renowned. All acknowledged Painter Chen as the master of all masters.

And it was as such that he was approached for a painting by a powerful magistrate. The magistrate did not recognize Painter Chen, but Liang recognized him as the young judge, now much older.

"Painter Chen," the magistrate said, "I commend you on your work on my son's project. The paintings in the Long Walkway are beautiful to behold."

"Thank you," Painter Chen said. "I still have much to do. I plan to paint every beam and ceiling placard."

The magistrate frowned as he watched the painter.

"You are painting that beam with water!" the magistrate said. "No one can see what you are painting if you paint with water!"

"They will see this painting when it is ready to be seen," Painter Chen said. "Was there something you wished to speak to me about?"

"Ah, yes," the magistrate said. "I would like to commission you to create a painting for my own palace."

Even though Painter Chen had misgivings, he made an agreement. The magistrate would forgo taxing

Painter Chen's old hometown village for a year and Painter Chen would paint the magistrate a dragon.

And his painting was magnificent. Per his custom, Painter Chen did not dot the eyes of the dragon and gave the unfinished painting to the magistrate. Unfortunately, back at his palace, the magistrate saw this error and attempted to fix the painting himself—which caused the dragon to come to life!

The dragon destroyed the magistrate's palace, causing chaos and calamity before disappearing. But the dragon's appearance made the magistrate realize Painter Chen's real identity. With his guards, he hastened to capture the artist.

In the meantime, Painter Chen was finishing the last painting on the Long Walkway. His apprentices ran to him with warnings, urging him to flee, but Painter Chen continued to calmly paint. When the Painter finally glanced away from his work, he saw the magistrate and his men rushing toward him, their swords drawn.

Without a word, Painter Chen turned back to his painting. It was a landscape scene, a calm blue sea and a distant land. With a few quick, sure strokes, he painted a boat in the water. Just as the tip of one of the men's swords was about to touch him, Painter Chen jumped right into the painting! All stared open-mouthed and shocked as Painter Chen sailed away in the painted boat to the painted land, taking his magic paintbrush with him.

"Ah, good story," said the stonecutter. "It's interesting how all the magistrates and king's fathers in your stories seem to have the same personality. It's as if they could all be the same person."

"It does seem that way, doesn't it?" Amah agreed.

"Though I suppose the powerful all seem the same to us," the stonecutter said, laughing, "All those characters could even be Our Exalted Majesty himself."

"Yes," Amah said. "They could."

CHAPTER
62

"Look!" Yishan said, pointing. "Something is happening!"

They had been walking toward the Capital City, the frozen sea looking exactly as before, even though the Sea King warned them that some time had passed, perhaps as much as three moon cycles. He had left them on the outskirts of the city after an incredible flight, not up to the surface of the sea as Pinmei had expected, but over the edge of the bridge and downward to the Heavenly Lake. The water had parted before them as they dove and the moon had grown bigger and bigger, becoming a giant hole in the star-spattered curtain of water that they burst through to arrive in the sky above the Capital City.

They had been walking in silence, for Pinmei was sulking—while she agreed about the tortoise, she was still angry at Yishan. He could have told her he was going to ask about the tortoise first! And the whole time he was at Sea Bottom, he had acted strangely. She was sure he was hiding something from her, and her irritation was just as visible as the clouds of steam from their warm breaths. Yishan, however, pretended not to notice, and was just about to suggest changing direction when an outpouring of people began to cluster into view. Great crowds were forming—women, children, men.

"Men!" Pinmei said, forgetting her annoyance. "There are men in the Capital City."

"Obviously," Yishan said, "the emperor only uses the men from the mountain villages for his slaves. Let's go see what the fuss is about."

Together, they ran toward the crowd. As they reached it, Pinmei tugged on the arm of an elderly woman. "What is happening?" she asked.

"It's the funeral, child!" the woman said, as if she should know.

"Whose funeral?" Yishan asked.

"Her husband's!" the woman replied, distracted. "They are starting the procession to the Grand Pier!"

"I heard the emperor himself will follow the coffin," another woman said, "wearing mourning robes!"

"Strange that they are burying him in the sea," another said. "I'd be afraid of the bad luck."

"She insisted," someone else said. "It was one of her conditions."

"How can they even put it in the sea?" a girl asked. "It's frozen!"

"Did you not hear them with the pickaxes this morning?" the first woman said. "Chop, chop, chopping for hours through the ice! Just so they can throw in the coffin! The emperor will do anything to get her to marry him."

"She must be very beautiful," said the girl. There was a hint of awe and envy in her voice.

"Oh, she is," one of the women said. "Remember how angry the emperor was after what she had done to his wall? But as soon as he saw her, he was enchanted."

"Who?" Yishan said, matching his steps with the group. "What did she do to the wall?"

"She destroyed it!" the first woman said, looking at Yishan. "Did you not hear the story?"

"Destroyed the Vast Wall?" Pinmei gasped.

"Well, only part of it," the woman conceded. "She was looking for her husband at the Vast Wall. She traveled a great distance, all on foot, with only a bundle of cloth…"

"I bet it was clothes for her husband," another interjected. "Someone said it was all embroidered…"

"But when she finally got to the wall, she was told her husband had died," the woman continued, ignoring the interruption. "And, in shock, she began to wail and wail and cursed the heavens, ten hundred tears pouring—"

"I was told she stood like a statue and shed only one tear," another person said.

"Well, a hundred tears or one," the woman said, obviously cross to have her account disputed, "when her tear fell on the wall, the part it touched just collapsed—as if crushed by her sorrow."

"And her husband's body was right there in the rubble," another woman added.

"So the emperor was angry and probably wanted to punish her, right?" Yishan said, prodding. "But when he saw her, he wanted to marry her?"

"And she wouldn't," the girl piped in. "Not unless he gave her husband a funeral that buried him in the sea."

"Which is what is happening now!" the first woman said, glaring at all the others.

In the distance, a faint, ponderous beating of drums called. Yishan looked at Pinmei, and without a word they began to run forward, bits of conversation dropping upon them with the snow.

"...four hundred *li* of the wall fell," one voice said as Yishan darted through a pack of people, "as if her tear knocked it down..."

"...thousands of bones under the wall," another voice said as Pinmei ducked underneath a gossiping couple.

"...it had to be clothes," another said as they pushed onto the Grand Pier, the broad platform stretching over silent waves of ice like an unfinished bridge. "She had the embroidered bundle put into the coffin with him..."

But then Pinmei's ears became deaf to all but the crashing sounds of cymbals and drums. Yishan grabbed Pinmei's arm and pulled her farther down the long pier ahead of them. As they neared the end, Pinmei could see the black gash of water where the ice had been chopped away. Imperial soldiers poured into the streets.

"Back!" a soldier barked as the soldiers lined up on either side of the pier. "Stand back!"

The crowd moved in a wave, pushing Pinmei and Yishan to the edge of the wharf. Pinmei looked over her shoulder nervously, eyeing the ice below.

"Kneel!" another soldier ordered as the pounding of drums became even louder. "All kneel as the emperor arrives!"

Everyone immediately obeyed. The sounds of the drums and cymbals boomed as the procession passed.

Pinmei peeked through the clumps of people in front of her. Funeral banners swayed before her, and farther away stood two figures shrouded with the pale coarse clothes of mourning. Pinmei thought the broad-shouldered man looked more annoyed than sad, his head bowed only the smallest fraction in respect for the dead. Yishan nudged her and Pinmei nodded back. They both knew it was the emperor.

The drums stopped beating and the cymbals made their final bang. For a moment there was no sound; even the wind was as silent as the trapped water below. There was the low murmuring of a priest as the pallbearers began to lower the coffin from their shoulders. As the mourners turned their backs to the coffin to await its burial, Pinmei could not help stealing a look.

For, as she suspected, standing next to the emperor in white funeral robes was Lady Meng.

CHAPTER
63

Lady Meng was as beautiful as ever. Even in funeral clothing, she looked as if she had been carved of ivory, the flower-petal fineness of all her features undiminished by the rough hemp robes. Delicate snowflakes fell upon her, and as she heard the splash of the coffin falling into the sea, Lady Meng raised her head. She gave the sky a small, sad smile, the same smile she had given Pinmei as they said farewell.

The emperor had already turned back around, eager for the burial to be completed. When he saw the coffin's absence, his back straightened and, saying something impossible for Pinmei to hear, took hold of Lady Meng's arm as if to take possession of her. Lady Meng flinched and pulled away, walking to the edge of the pier to look down into the black water.

"It is done," the emperor said, this time his voice loud enough for all to hear.

Lady Meng turned around and slowly lifted her head—her neck rising to a proud, defiant arch. The wind began to blow again, a low, angry howl.

"Come!" the emperor demanded, beckoning with his arm.

"I will not come," Lady Meng said. Her voice was low, her words cutting into the air.

"I have done as you asked!" the emperor said. "Do you not remember?"

"I said I could only marry after my husband was buried," Lady Meng said.

"And now he is buried," the emperor said, "and you are to be my wife."

"Marry you?" Lady Meng said, her eyes glittering. "A ruthless tyrant who does not care who suffers for him? Never!"

"You will marry me!" the emperor said, his voice dangerous. He began to stalk toward her, snowflakes whipping around him in a mad frenzy.

"You may try," Lady Meng said, speaking the words as if spitting poison, "to marry my corpse."

Then, in a single, swift motion, she jumped into the black water.

"No!" Pinmei's scream was lost in the gasps of horror from the crowd. Everyone pushed forward, the people to gape and the guards to act as the emperor bellowed, "Get her! She is not to get away!"

But those at the edge of the pier halted, bewildered at what they saw below. As those unable to see clamored with questions, agitated shouts and murmurs of wonder resounded. "The water has frozen over!" someone screeched. "The hole has closed!"

"Break the ice!" the emperor ordered. "I want her found!"

Confusion shook the pier, but in mere seconds, pickaxes and men were lowering onto the refrozen ice. The throngs of people, all in an uproar, pressed forward for a better view. Pinmei, at the rear, saw only a forest of legs and backs of coats and robes. As she jumped and leaned, the cries and shouts of the crowd echoing around her, Yishan grabbed her arm.

"Look," he said quietly, pulling her back.

He pointed at the ice below. Pinmei peered below and

gasped, the sound swallowed by the roar of the spectacle behind them. As everyone else was facing the opposite direction, no one noticed what they saw.

Under the surface of the ice was the translucent figure of someone swimming. Even though scarcely a shadow, the silhouette was graceful and lithe, her hair streaming behind her like ripples in the water. But what made Pinmei gape was that as the woman turned to swim away, she distinctly flipped the tail of a fish.

CHAPTER
64

He only shrieked now when he woke. The ache of his lost dreams would pierce him, and the dazzling gold mocked him.

How he longed for his serene blackness! How he longed for his clean, clear waves of water! The weight on his back was nothing compared with the weight of his longing.

When he was finally free, how he would race back! He would trample anything in his way, toss aside anyone in his path. Nothing would slow him—no mountain or immortal, no building or beast.

Not even the human who had captured him.

For he found he did not care about his power, his strength, or his greatness. He did not care about finding his captor, repaying insults, or inflicting eternal punishments.

Vindication, vengeance, revenge. He no longer wished for those things.

He wished for tranquil darkness patterned with gentle ripples and delicate lights. He wished for his limbs to swim in cold, deep wetness. He wished for the sound of clear wind, free and boundless.

His only wish was to return home.

CHAPTER
65

"So we'll save Amah when we find the Iron Rod," Yishan said, "and free the tortoise."

"We wouldn't have to do anything with the tortoise if you hadn't pretended we were the people the Sea King had called!" Pinmei said, scowling, her anger returning. "Were you even pretending? Why did you act that way?"

They were at an inn, the steam from the warm tea in their hands drifting with the drafts from the window. They had gotten a room as well as dinner, though the innkeeper had raised his eyebrows as the children had entered. However, his face settled back into businesslike detachment when Yishan reached into his bag and waved a gold coin. "Just a present from the House of Wu," Yishan had told Pinmei when she looked at him, her own eyebrows lifted.

"Listen," Yishan said, ignoring Pinmei's questions, "we know that the emperor has captured the tortoise with the Iron Rod..."

"So that he can be invincible," Pinmei put in, "which usually means impossible to beat."

"He'd want to keep the tortoise close to him," continued Yishan, as if Pinmei hadn't spoken. "I can't imagine anything being able to hold in the tortoise forever. Even with the Iron Rod, the emperor must know that the tortoise might be able to break free at any time. What kind of cage could hold the Black Tortoise of Winter, though?"

"Maybe it's made of mountains," Pinmei said with bitterness. "The emperor probably had some built in his throne room."

Yishan's eyes widened, and he stared out the window at the dimming sky as if suddenly seeing the sun.

"Of course," he said. "That's why he's building the wall! It's to keep the tortoise in, if he should ever break free. He's probably reinforcing it with..."

"Yishan!" Pinmei almost screamed, her frustration

finally bursting. "Just tell me what's really going on! You're hiding things from me."

"I'm not!" Yishan said, smiling innocently. "At least not anything important."

Pinmei looked at him with narrowed eyes, suspicious as well as angry. How could he smile like that? Couldn't he see how impossible he had made things? Find the Iron Rod! Free the Black Tortoise! Was it for a secret reason of his own that he went to Sea Bottom? And he and Lady Meng had always acted a bit strange with each other. Maybe there had been hidden reasons for him to find the stone too! Had he even wanted to save Amah in the first place? Pinmei's eyes burned with tears, and the wind shrieked as the night darkened the sky, the paper of the window flapping.

"Pinmei," Yishan said again, but this time his voice was no longer pleading, but deep and clear with unexpected gravity. "Trust me."

Remember, you can always trust Yishan, Amah had said. Pinmei bowed her head, remembering Amah's gentle but firm voice. Her frustrated tears transformed into tears of yearning as she pictured Amah's face looking at her steadily, like the light of the clear moon. Would she ever see her again? Pinmei let the tears fall down her cheeks before opening her eyes. She looked at Yishan and saw the boy who had pulled her out of a fiery hut and away from the hands of a cruel soldier. No matter what, he was her true friend. She let out a slow breath and nodded. He could keep his secrets if he wanted.

"So, the Iron Rod, the tortoise, Amah," Pinmei said slowly, wiping her face with her hand. "The emperor has them all. They must all be in the palace. That means we have to get in there. How are we going to do that?"

Yishan grinned and took his handkerchief out of his sleeve, holding it out to her as he had to Lady Meng so long ago. "We'll think of something," he said. "You always—"

"Yishan!" Pinmei gasped. "Your handkerchief... *Look!*"

"What?" Yishan stared at Pinmei. Her face had turned white and her black eyes burned. Both her eyes and her hand, frozen in pointing, were fixed on Yishan's outstretched handkerchief.

"What is it?" Yishan started, but stopped as he followed Pinmei's gaze. In his humble handkerchief lay a small, round stone. Exquisite in its size, perfect in its shape, the stone was lovelier than the finest pearl and more gorgeous than the costliest jewel.

"You let Lady Meng use that handkerchief," Pinmei whispered, "when she cried..."

Yishan continued to stare, his mouth and eyes as round as the object in his hand. For once, he was completely silent.

"It's her tear!" Pinmei stuttered. "She...she's the Sea King's daughter...a goddess with a fish tail...and this is...it's...it's..."

As she stammered, the last of the sun died away and night took its place, the flame of their lantern flickering. But the light in the room was steady and bright. For the precious stone had begun to glow a soft, serene radiance just like the moon.

"A Luminous Stone That Lights the Night!" Pinmei breathed.

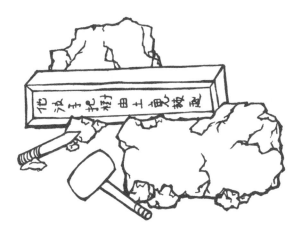

CHAPTER

66

"Stonecutter!" a voice boomed.

Amah and the stonecutter flinched. The voice had roared out of the shadows, giving both the unsettling feeling they were about to be pounced upon. And when the guards emerged from the darkness, Amah felt her throat tighten. She recognized one of them as the soldier in green from so long ago—the same soldier she knew was not a soldier, any more than he was a guard now.

"I have come to see your work!" he bellowed.

The stonecutter jumped up, carrying an armful of stones to the guard. But as he brought them closer, he froze, staring at the face of the guard. The stones in his arms began to clink together as his arms trembled.

Amah quickly took some stones from the stonecutter and brought them to the guard.

"There are still many more to cut," Amah said.

The man took one of the stones. As he inspected it, Amah wondered: Why did the emperor disguise himself as a lowly guard? Was it the only way to come to the dungeon without causing attention? But why would the emperor even wish to come to the dungeon? Was it for the stonecutter? Or was it for her?

Suddenly, he glowered at Amah. "Why do you look at me like that?" the emperor barked.

Amah lowered her head. "I'm sorry," she said. "You reminded me of someone."

"Who?" he demanded.

"Just someone in a story," Amah said.

"A story, of course," the emperor said with irritation. "Very well. Tell it."

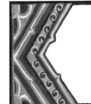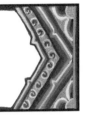

THE STORY OF THE
THREE EVILS

Once there was a man named Haiyi who was as strong as a dragon and bigger than an ox. But he was also as wild and as unpredictable as a tiger. When he walked down the street, villagers fled and quickly shut their doors. For Haiyi caused chaos wherever he went. Because of his great strength, he just took what he wished, and none dared oppose him. He spent his time drinking and gambling.

One night, he stumbled out of the village in a drunken daze, lifting his wine bottle to the moon.

"Am I not the greatest man who has ever lived?" he called out. "Is this not the happiest village, for I am in it?"

"If it were not for three things," a calm, clear voice said at his knee, "this village would indeed be happy."

Haiyi looked down, slightly dizzy, and saw an old man sitting in the light of the moon, a large book in his lap.

"It's the Old Man of the Moon!" Haiyi boomed. "Have you come to see Haiyi, the great hero?"

"You would have to rid the village of its three evils," the Old Man of the Moon said, "before you could be called a great hero."

Haiyi felt his drunkenness fade as he stared into the steady black eyes of the Old Man of the Moon. "Three evils?" Haiyi asked as he sat.

"Yes," the Old Man replied. "As I said, if it were not for the three evils plaguing the village, this village would indeed be happy."

"What are they?" Haiyi asked.

"The first evil," the Old Man said, "is the Bashe snake. It lives underneath the Black Bridge. When a man or beast passes him, he swallows it whole."

Haiyi rose. "I will slay this beast," he declared. "And then you may tell me the second evil."

With that, he rushed to the Black Bridge. The bridge had long been abandoned, and when he finally reached it, the Bashe immediately rose from the water. It reared against the dark sky, its hideous, gaping mouth wide enough to swallow an entire elephant. Haiyi dodged the swooping jaws and dove into the river. For a moment, all was still, but then the river began to churn, bubbling with a foul odor. Finally, one enormous wave flew into the sky and crashed down again—the water scattering like shattered pieces of stone. When at last the water calmed, a bright red stain floated to the surface—growing larger until the entire river was red. And then Haiyi burst through the water, gasping. In one hand, he held his sword, and in the other, the head of the Bashe snake.

That night, Haiyi returned to the Old Man of the Moon.

"I have slain the Bashe snake," Haiyi said. "Now there are only two evils plaguing the village."

"The second evil," the Old Man of the Moon said, "is the Noxious Zhen bird that lives on Northern Mountain. It drinks the venom of vipers, so its feathers are pure poison. Its blood can melt stone, and its saliva dissolves steel."

"I will be back tomorrow to hear the third evil," Haiyi said, and he turned toward Northern Mountain. On his way, he stopped and changed into robes of thick leather. He also took a large hide of rhinoceros, some raw meat, and a strong rope.

He climbed to the top of the mountain and waved the piece of raw meat. The Zhen bird, smelling the meat, dove at Haiyi, who quickly placed a noose around its neck. The bird screeched and flew upward, carrying

Haiyi into the sky. But he refused to let go and instead pulled the noose tighter until the Zhen, unable to breathe, fell to the ground.

Haiyi, after landing on the ground himself, ran to the fallen bird. He gave the noose a final pull, breaking the bird's neck. He then took out the rhinoceros hide, wrapped the bird inside it and burned the whole thing.

The Old Man of the Moon was waiting for him when Haiyi returned at night.

"I have destroyed the Zhen bird," Haiyi said, "so the villagers no longer need to fear its poison."

"Yes," the Old Man said.

"And I killed the Bashe snake," Haiyi said, "so the villagers can now travel on the Black Bridge safely."

"Yes," the Old Man said.

"So the first two evils are no longer," Haiyi said.

"Yes," the Old Man said. "Now there is only one evil left that plagues the village."

"What is it?" Haiyi said. "I shall end it as I did the others."

The Old Man of the Moon looked at Haiyi, his black eyes piercing.

"The third and last evil plaguing the village," the Old Man of the Moon said, "is you."

"Nonsense!" the emperor snorted. "What a ridiculous story!"

"Is it?" Amah said. "Haiyi did not think so. When he was told that he himself was the final evil, he bowed his head in shame, and tears began to flow from his eyes."

"Weak fool," the emperor spat.

"He left the village to rid it of its last evil," Amah continued, "and reformed, lived a life of peace, and then, at last, was a great hero."

"He killed the snake and the poison-feather bird!" the emperor said. "His deeds were great! He was already a great hero!"

"His deeds were great," Amah said. "But, no, he was not a hero. Not then."

The emperor stared at Amah, his expression slowly transforming into a glare. He dropped the stone and turned, the other guard quickly moving to follow.

"That woman is never to speak in my presence again!" the emperor snarled. He stormed away, the echo of his roar locked in the dungeon with Amah and the stonecutter.

CHAPTER
67

Even with the Luminous Stone, it was not easy to see the emperor. At first, the guards at the gate ignored them, and when they finally acknowledged Yishan's persistent requests, they did little more than pass the message on to a servant. To the guards' amusement, the children camped out by the gate, waiting for a response.

"Go home," one of them said. "Do you really think you are going to be let into the Imperial Palace?"

"When the emperor hears we have the Luminous Stone," Yishan said, "he'll let us in. He'll want to see us."

"See you! The emperor?" the other soldier said, laughing coarsely. "Even I have never met with the emperor! How would two little beggars like you meet with him?"

Yishan said no more, but as the morning turned to afternoon and started toward evening, Pinmei felt her hopes dip with the sun. But just as the sky began to darken, an imperial servant arrived.

"The children who say they have the Luminous Stone That Lights the Night," he said, looking at Yishan and Pinmei huddled in the corner, "is that you two?"

They jumped up, nodding.

"Come!" the servant said. "The emperor wants to see you."

The waiting guards said nothing, but their eyes bulged like crickets' as the children passed. "Goodbye, gentlemen," Yishan said with a wink, and Pinmei marveled at his composure. They were going to the Imperial Palace! They were going to see the emperor! She could scarcely breathe.

They stepped out into the immense courtyard with red walls and columns, carved green and gold. Five marble bridges lay ahead of them, their jutting posts like bones of a skeleton. As they walked over one of the bridges, Pinmei looked down and saw a fish trapped in the ice. She shivered.

They passed through another elaborate gate and courtyard, their footsteps the only sound in the emptiness.

Ahead, a commanding gold-topped building of blood-red loomed before them.

"Come," the servant said with impatience as Pinmei stopped to stare. The building, everything inside the imperial gates, was cold and imposing.

Pinmei gulped, but Yishan nudged her. "I like the Sea King's palace better," he said. "More light, lots of colors—this is a bit off-putting, don't you think?"

Pinmei gave Yishan a weak smile and shook her head, but her awe lessened. Her dread, however, remained. Her knees shook as they climbed the tiered staircase, the carved dragons frozen on their ramps of marble slabs. The servant continued forward to push open the studded crimson doors.

In front of them was the emperor.

CHAPTER
68

He was like the sun, sitting above them and dazzling in his gold robes. All around were red columns, decorated ceilings, court attendants, and guards, but Pinmei noticed none of those. All she saw were the emperor's piercing black eyes. They were the same eyes that Pinmei had seen through the crack in the *gang* so long ago. She would have stood there gaping, but the servant shoved her as he himself bent over. "Kneel!" he ordered.

Pinmei fell to the ground, letting her forehead touch the cold floor. She sneaked a glance at Yishan. He too had gotten on his knees, but his head was bowed only slightly, his eyes scanning the room. Pinmei knew he was hoping for a hint of the Black Tortoise.

The emperor waved his hand with impatience. "Have you a Luminous Stone That Lights the Night?" he said, the eagerness straining through his voice.

Yishan straightened. "Yes," he said in his confident way, and he patted his pocket.

"We'll give it to you in exchange," Pinmei said, trying to speak as boldly as Yishan. She clenched her fists to hide their trembling. "For my grandmother."

"And who is your grandmother?" the emperor said.

"She is the Storyteller," Pinmei said, and, despite her efforts, her voice sounded thin in the echoing room.

"Ahh," the emperor said, sitting back. "The Storyteller."

"Yes," Pinmei said, and her anger gave her voice the volume she had been trying for. "You took her from our mountain hut."

"Did I?" the emperor said. His mouth curved into an amused smile, but his eyes remained fixed upon them.

"Let me see the stone," the emperor said. Pinmei looked at Yishan.

"Let us see the Storyteller," Yishan said, nodding at her. The room murmured with gasps.

The emperor laughed, a harsh, unkind noise. "Very

well," he said, and he sat up and looked at the window. A faint light streamed through the carved openings, causing a decoration on the emperor's collar to flash in Pinmei's eyes. She squinted, a vague memory flicking past her as the emperor continued, "We cannot test the stone in the day, in any case."

"We will wait for night in the courtyard of the Hall of Imperial Longevity," he said, standing and causing all the attendants to rush forward in a flutter. "That will be fitting."

"My grandmother?" Pinmei inquired.

The emperor waved his hands impatiently at one of the guards. "Get the old woman," he barked, "and bring her through the Black Tortoise Gate."

CHAPTER
69

The emperor's attendants and guards flapped and scattered in a large wave. From nowhere, a large, elaborate sedan chair was brought forward, which the emperor settled into with great comfort. "Food and wine!" he ordered before closing the thick drapes. "It may be some time before nightfall, and I get hungry in the cold."

Countless servants rushed ahead, carrying ornamental lanterns and heaters. Bodyguards stood on either side of the sedan, and swaying ladies of the court trailed at the back. Pinmei and Yishan found themselves behind the sedan carriers, surrounded by the emperor's entourage.

They walked silently out of the hall, a grand procession in the snow.

Just as the emperor was being carried over the last carved ramp, a servant came running up with a large, steaming bamboo basket. He thrust the container between the curtains of the chair and, after a bark from the emperor, jumped into the chair himself.

"Food taster," Yishan whispered to Pinmei, who watched the proceedings with confusion. "For poison!"

Pinmei nodded. *He doesn't trust anyone*, Pinmei realized. *Everyone is an enemy.* Unexpectedly, she felt a pang of pity.

Lost in these thoughts, Pinmei scarcely noticed how long they walked or where they were going. Everything was bleak and grim; even the red of the palace walls were cold.

As they approached another gate, Yishan nudged her. "The Black Tortoise Gate," he said, giving her a look. She scanned the area, but she saw nothing, only the same scarlet walls and white snow.

However, after they passed through the gate, Pinmei realized they were now in the Imperial Garden. In front of them, flanking the courtyard, plants and trees slept under their thick blankets of snow. All was still and silent except for a quick, high movement of a monkey tail disappearing in the shadow of the pines.

"Stop here!" the emperor's voice barked out from the sedan chair. As the procession stopped and the chair was lowered, the emperor called out again. "The children with the stone! Where are they?"

The guards shoved them forward and all dropped onto their knees in the cold snow as the emperor pushed open the drapes of his sedan chair. He was chewing a dumpling, silver chopsticks in one hand and a bowl in the other. When Pinmei raised her head, a shock ran through her. The bowl in his hand was Amah's special rice bowl! The rabbit rice bowl he had taken from their hut! Any pity Pinmei had felt disappeared, her eyes now flashing.

But before Pinmei could do more than scowl, there was movement at the gate. Three people were walking toward them. Two were soldiers, each gripping the arm of the small, shuffling figure in the middle. Pinmei felt as if she were breathing jade stones. For, even from a distance, she knew who the third person was.

Amah.

CHAPTER
70

Amah was thinner and grayer, her robe dirty and stained. However, even as she staggered through the snow, her back was straight and her head, high. As she came closer, Pinmei's anger reignited, for Amah had a white cloth tied around her mouth. They had gagged her! But Pinmei stayed silent, for above the gag, Amah's eyes flashed frantic warnings at her. What was wrong? What was Amah trying to say?

"Ah, the Storyteller has arrived," the emperor said. He looked at Yishan and said, "The stone?"

Yishan took his handkerchief from his sleeve and opened it. The emperor leaned forward, and the crowd murmured. The stone seemed to reflect all the splendors of the world: the glittering of the sun on the sea, the flickering of fire, and the shine of silken threads.

The emperor sat back as if satisfied. "Now," he said, picking up his bowl and chopsticks again, "we wait for night."

He waved his hand and an attendant laid more dishes on a small lacquered table. The scent of bird's nest with smoked chicken, meat-stuffed peaches, and wine-stewed pork floated in the air. Pinmei heard Yishan's stomach grumble.

The emperor inserted his silver chopsticks in the dishes several times, inspecting the chopsticks after each jab. As he bent, the glint from his collar caught Pinmei's eye again. What was it? Like a tiny fish, a thought wavered in her mind—only to swim away as the emperor sat up and grunted. As the waiting servant began to taste each of his dishes, the emperor looked again at Pinmei and Yishan.

"This is a good time for a story," the emperor said with an unkind smile. "Too bad the Storyteller is a bit limited right now."

"You could take her gag off," Yishan said. He too had noticed the alarm in Amah's eyes.

"I think not," the emperor said. "It's best not to underestimate the power of the Storyteller's voice." He filled the white-rabbit rice bowl with noodles, the long strips hanging from his chopsticks like limp threads. "But you," the emperor continued, looking at Pinmei, "you must know a story of your grandmother's. You tell one."

Pinmei looked at him, his black eyes mocking and triumphant, and she felt something deeper than rage steel itself inside her. "I can tell you a story," Pinmei said, her voice as hard as iron, "but it is not one of my grandmother's."

"Better!" the emperor said. "Hers are tiresome."

"This one won't be," Pinmei said, her eyes the sparks of heated metal. "It's never been heard before."

"Good," the emperor said. "Begin!"

THE STORY OF OUR MOUNTAIN

The mountain we are from has been called many names—Endless Mountain, Moon-Holding Peak, even Never-Ending Mountain. They say the earth, the sea, and the heavens meet at the tip of it, and it is there that the moon rests.

Also at the top of the mountain is supposed to be an old man, a man who too has many names. They have called him the Wise Sage, the Spirit of the Mountain, and the Old Man of the Moon.

Because of this, our mountain is sacred. It is tradition for newly made rulers to come and pay tribute to it. They are supposed to climb to the top of the mountain to meet with the Mountain Spirit, to gain his wisdom and approval, and, by doing so, to prove they are the fated ruler. Many have come and claimed to have climbed to the top, but we who live in the middle of the mountain have not yet looked up at any of them.

Some we do not even get to look down at, for they never even reach halfway. But even though we do not see them, we hear about them. Perhaps the Mountain Spirit whispers in our dreams, or maybe the moon cannot help showing us when we close our eyes.

Such is the story of the last ruler who tried to visit our mountain. This ruler began his trip after the start of the winter, a winter that came early and harshly with winds that whipped and screamed at the mountain peak. When his ministers timidly suggested waiting until spring, he refused.

"I want everyone to see I am the destined ruler," he said, lifting his head above them, his gaze toward the sky. "Even the Old Man of the Moon."

So, in his best-built sedan chair and with his strongest servants and warmest furs, the new ruler traveled to the mountain. By the time they arrived at the village at the foot of the mountain, all the horses were spent and the servants exhausted. They were all grateful that tradition called for the ruler to mount the cliff alone, for the mountain can only use its powers for one person at a time.

And so he began to climb. But as soon as he was out of sight, gusts of wind and snow, as if kicked from the stone beneath, flew up at him. He was struck and slapped with small, sharp pebbles, and the snow blinded him. He tried to continue, stumbling and thrashing, but a large rock tripped him and he found himself sprawled on the ground. As he sat himself up, he heard laughing. He glanced around quickly, his hand on his sword, but saw only rock and snow.

"You dare laugh at me?" the man shouted. "Do you know who I am?"

"I do," a mocking voice said in his ear. The man whirled around but again saw nothing. "But do you know who you are?"

"Of course!" the man retorted, drawing his sword.

"Do you?" the voice teased. "Were you a man transformed into a green tiger or were you a green tiger that was transformed into a man? Will you ever know?"

The man bellowed his fury and swung his sword into swirling snow, only to hear laughter again in his ear.

"Trying to fight the snow?" the voice mocked him. "You best get used to it! You are stuck with winter until you let go of the Black Tortoise."

The ruler swung his sword in the other direction, squinting through the threads of snow.

"You poor mortal," the voice said with contempt.

"Poor!" the man shouted, outraged. "I am not poor!"

"You are so poor you had to steal a bite of a long-life peach," the voice said in scorn. "And even that was not enough for you. The Iron Rod, the power of the Black Tortoise…what else have you stolen?"

"Everything is mine!" the man shouted. "I am ruler!"

"You are a thief," the voice said in disdain. "Poor mortal."

"I am ruler!" the man bellowed. "That is who I am!"

But his words were thrown away by the wind. "Poor mortal," the voice whispered, and the stone under his feet jerked and jolted, flinging him down again. The mountain seemed to swell and break, tossing the man so he reeled and rolled. "Poor mortal," the mountain murmured. The words repeated again and again, twisting inside his head as he fell. Finally, the ground stopped moving, and the mountain gave one last faded whisper. "Poor mortal."

The ruler sat up. He was at the foot of the mountain. His servants and a crowd of villagers surrounded him, staring. He glared and ordered that they return him to his palace immediately.

He was soon in his sedan chair, his servants carrying him again on the arduous road. "The tortoise must never escape," they heard him mutter to himself as they panted. "I can surround it with stone, just in case it slips the Iron Rod...reinforce it with great deeds... I will not be a poor mortal!"

And when they reached the palace, even before he had stepped out from behind the curtains of the sedan, the ruler was already calling out orders.

"I want a wall built," he said. "A stone wall around the entire kingdom, with special reinforcements I will oversee."

"A wall of that size…" one of the ministers began, and stopped in nervousness.

"It's for protection," the ruler said, his eyes dangerous. "Begin at once."

And so it was done. Work began on the wall, a wall so vast it could span the sea. Mountain villagers, as if being punished for the ruler's humiliation, were forced to work on it—many dying in the harsh cold. But no one dared to complain or protest. For after the ruler had returned from the mountain, all finally saw the madness in him. It was a cruel, ruthless madness, and it made them shiver more than a bitter, endless winter.

The emperor stood, shoving aside his bowl and chopsticks. The small table fell, the crashing and shattering of dishes making Pinmei jump. Everyone except Yishan fell to their knees as the emperor pushed his way off the sedan chair, his eyes glittering.

"That was quite an interesting story," the emperor said, his voice dangerous.

Pinmei felt her words disappear. The emperor was moving closer, like a stalking animal. His eyes pierced hers, and Pinmei began to tremble.

"Tell me," the emperor said, "is that the end?"

Pinmei opened her mouth, but instead of speaking, she stared. For in the falling light, she could see what had glinted from the emperor's collar. She had seen it before, under the emperor's green soldier's uniform. That metal pin! Now Pinmei could see it was sticking out of some sort of dark embroidered image. Was it a...

"Because," the emperor said with the beginning of an ominous roar, "I think you..."

But he stopped, for a silver light began to shine upon him. The emperor switched his gaze to Yishan, or rather to Yishan's upheld hands. Just as if he were cupping the moon, a clear, soft brightness spilled from his hands and poured into the sky. The Luminous Stone was lighting the night.

"It glows!" the emperor said, his eyes widening. "It is the stone!"

The crowd gasped and, as the guards loosened their hold, Amah yanked off the gag. "Yishan! Pinmei!" she cried out. "He doesn't want the stone! It's a trap!"

CHAPTER
71

The guards growled, and one of them struck Amah a brutal blow. She crumpled to the ground. Pinmei screamed, and her scream froze in the air, along with her legs.

The emperor laughed, a cruel, cold laugh that filled the sky.

"She's right!" he said to them as his laughter echoed. "I never wanted the stone!"

The emperor was looking at Yishan with malicious triumph, an almost hungry look in his eyes.

"It was you!" the emperor said. "It was you I wanted

all this time! I knew only you could bring me the stone, Ginseng Boy!"

Ginseng Boy? Pinmei whisked her head to look, open-mouthed, at Yishan. He was staring back at the emperor in shock and, for the first time Pinmei could remember, she saw a flicker of fear on Yishan's face. Pinmei suddenly felt as if she were seeing him for the first time, the redness of Yishan's hat and clothes burning with a light of its own.

"Old Man of the Moon! Spirit of the Mountain! Whatever they call you!" the emperor continued. "You, who can never ignore mortal suffering! You, who always come to help! That's how I knew you would come! And now that I have you, I will have my immortality!"

"No!" Yishan hissed, and he threw the stone at the emperor. For a moment, the world silenced. The stone flew in a direct arc toward the emperor's chest, like a shooting star in the dark sky. The emperor's eyes flashed in the light of the lanterns, showing sudden terror. But right before the stone hit, out of nowhere, a black shadow jumped in and seized it!

The shadow fell to the ground with a thud so hard the stones beneath it cracked, and Pinmei saw the shadow was a monkey. The ugly creature was on its back with its arms and legs flailing, but unable to move because of the weight of the stone on his chest. He was spitting and sputtering, and another monkey, a green bracelet around its arm gleaming in the light, scrambled to it. The second monkey struggled and hissed, trying to lift the stone, but it could no more move it than it could move the moon.

The emperor laughed again and waved his hand. In an instant, the guards piled atop Yishan, his red hat disappearing from view.

"Here, only a mountain can lift the moon!" the emperor cackled. He began to stalk toward the hill of soldiers, his hand reaching for his sword. "The moon that is a tear cried by a fish-tail goddess! The tear that is stone that only you as the Mountain Spirit can carry! And you, as the Ginseng Boy, who I will kill to be immortal!"

"*No!*" Pinmei screamed. This time her scream released her legs, and she flew at the emperor. But his arms simply grabbed her as if scooping up a mound of snow, and his cruel laughter boomed in her ears.

However, instead of kicking and thrashing, Pinmei clutched at the emperor's golden robes, searching. Where was it? There! There it was! It wasn't a pin after all! It was a needle! A needle sticking into black embroidery. Black embroidery of a tortoise!

Her glimmering thought now sparked and flared. *The*

Iron Rod can shrink to the size of a needle, the Sea King had said. *I gave her that needle from the treasury*, Joy to the Heart had said. *I sewed him a dragon shirt to protect him, even leaving in my needle*, said Lady Meng. *The Tiger King held the piece of shirt in his hands*, the king of the City of Bright Moonlight said, and then *became invincible*. Pinmei stared at the needle. Could it? Could it be? It had to be!

So, with the emperor's laughter still echoing across the courtyard, Pinmei grabbed the needle and yanked the Iron Rod off the Black Tortoise of Winter.

CHAPTER
72

The sky bellowed.

It was a deafening noise, and those who were not already on the ground were knocked to their knees. Pinmei fell also, her fingers still clutching the needle, its point brandished toward the emperor like a sword. The unraveled black thread of the embroidered turtle stretched between them and melted away into the dark sky like a thin wisp of smoke. The emperor stared in disbelief.

But that was all he could do. An enormous burst of wind and winter ripped through the heavens. Pinmei flew forward, the power of it shoving her to her hands and knees, still clutching the needle, its point wedged into the mosaic stones of the courtyard. Between the thunderous roars of the wind, Pinmei heard screams and shouts and the chaos of fleeing figures. The earth seemed to be cresting a gigantic wave, throwing everyone around her like shaken droplets of water.

The sedan chair splintered into pieces, and lanterns were scattered. Oil and flames were flung across the courtyard, and flowers of fire bloomed from the frozen earth. Trees bowed in deep kowtows or broke their backs, a series of snaps like firecrackers popping, until one loud, sickening crack added to the cacophony in the sky.

Pinmei raised her head and watched in horror. A gigantic, invisible force was crushing the Black Tortoise Gate. The grand gate tore apart as if made of paper, scattering tiles and stone on the earth like sudden rain. The emperor was tossed forward and backward, his robe making him look like a golden ingot being juggled. Finally, he crashed against the largest column of the gate just as it collapsed. It fell to the ground, and the emperor disappeared beneath it. An inhuman howl, full of pain and resentment and anger, cut through the bellowing wind. The awful sound echoed and reverberated so much that even the stars seemed to shiver. A huge cloud of black dust swelled into the sky, and even the moon ceased to exist.

But in the darkness, Pinmei saw the faint red glow of the thread around her wrist. Her fingers still held the needle, its point embedded in the ground, the only ground that was unmoving and unshaken. The light from the thread spread down to the needle and over her arm, covering her entirely. She heard the shards of tile, torn branches, and slivers of wood pounding against the stone courtyard like the beating of drums, but nothing touched her. "The thread," she whispered. "It's protecting me and the needle is keeping this ground still."

A great gust split through the cloud, the black dust disintegrating into the night sky. The full moon burst through the darkness, brighter and more brilliant than before. Its light cascaded upon the earth like the divine glory of a goddess, and the world was silent again.

CHAPTER
73

It was a soft silence. The wind and the sky had finally quieted, and it was not the tense, anticipating stillness of winter, the pause of the tortoise taking a breath before a thunderous howl. No, it was the calm, grateful quiet of one seeing a friend return home.

Pinmei stood. The moon above spread its light generously, muting the ruins and wreckage. But Pinmei did not notice, for moonlight also fell upon a small, fragile figure crumpled in heap not far from her.

"Amah!" The name tore from Pinmei's throat, and she fell to her knees next to the fallen form. Amah's eyes were closed, her arms outstretched as if reaching. "Amah?" Pinmei said again, this time in a coarse, cracked whisper.

Amah did not move. She was as still as a clay figure. The only color to her ashen face was the dark trickle of blood from an ugly cut on her forehead. Pinmei threw herself against Amah's chest. "Amah! Amah!" she repeated desperately, willing her to awaken, but Amah was deaf to her pleas. Pinmei began to weep. Had she left the mountain for this? Had she borne the cold, run from soldiers, gone through the frozen sea, and fought the emperor for this? She wept heartbroken tears, tears as inconsolable as Lady Meng's and as despairing as Nuwa's.

"Pinmei," a voice said, and a hand touched her shoulder. She looked up and, through her tears, she saw Yishan.

He was bareheaded and his face was dirty, but he was unscathed, standing before her with an object in his hands. At first, Pinmei thought it was his hat, but as she blinked away more tears, she saw it was Amah's special rabbit rice bowl.

Yishan knelt next to her and placed his hand on Amah's chest. He drew it away swiftly and held his hand out to Pinmei.

"The Iron Rod," he said, in a tone so urgent Pinmei's tears stopped flowing. "Quickly!"

Pinmei handed Yishan the needle. He looked at her, and the corner of his mouth curved up in a smile. He reached out and gave her braid an affectionate tug.

Without a word, he pricked his finger and held it above the bowl. Only a single drop of clear, golden liquid fell from his finger, but when Pinmei looked into the bowl, it was full. He brought the bowl to Amah's lips, letting the liquid drip into her mouth.

Little by little, Amah's face began to color, the gray waxen tinge warming to rose gold. The evil gash on her temple disappeared as if wiped away, the stains of blood nothing more than dried paint. Her chest began to move with rhythmic breathing, and, slowly, very slowly, Amah opened her eyes.

She looked directly at Pinmei, and the love and longing Pinmei had carried for so long melted in her like a piece of ice in warm tea. Amah reached up and pulled Pinmei toward her. "My brave girl," Amah said. Pinmei began to weep again, but this time the tears were ones of happiness.

CHAPTER
74

After hugging Pinmei, Amah sat up and, to Pinmei's surprise, a sad expression came over her face.

"Yishan," Amah said, sitting up and shaking her head, "Meiya would never forgive me."

Pinmei turned to look at Yishan, and her mouth fell open. Yishan was not there. Instead, there was an old man, tall and silver and dressed in gray. He held a red bag in his hand, a bag Pinmei recognized as made from the same cloth as Yishan's clothes. She stared as the moon bathed him in its luminous light and he seemed to glow.

"She wanted you to finally live as a boy and grow old as

you are supposed to," Amah lamented, "instead of always giving up your youth to keep her alive. You shouldn't have done it for me."

"Nonsense, Minli," the old man said. He shook the needle in his hand, and it grew into an iron walking stick. "You know this is exactly what she would have wished me to do. Besides, what is another ninety-nine years? I'll soon be young again and I'll start over."

Pinmei's eyes bulged as she glanced back and forth between her grandmother and the old man. Yishan had turned into an old man because he saved Amah? He had done it before with Auntie Meiya?

"Yishan?" Pinmei started doubtfully.

"I never realized how short you are," he said, and the half-amused, half-serious black eyes she knew so well looked down at her from his wrinkled face. As impossible as it seemed, this old man was Yishan.

"I guess," she said unsteadily, "I guess this is what you were hiding from me?"

He gave a wide smile, and she was surprised again, for it was Yishan's grin on the old man's face. "I told you it wasn't anything important," he said.

He turned away and, with the Iron Rod, knocked over a small glowing light at the ground near their feet. Two monkeys popped up, whimpering and sobbing. The old man bent down, grabbed something, and then in a sharp voice said, "Go! And stay out of mischief!"

The monkeys ran off into the darkness, and the old man began to pick his way through the ruins of the courtyard, with Pinmei and Amah following. He stopped in front of the fallen column of the Black Tortoise Gate and, as if he were brushing away a dead leaf, pushed it aside.

"Amah," Pinmei said, finally recovering from her shock, "why didn't you tell me?"

"Well," Amah said gravely, motioning toward the ground near Yishan, "that is one reason."

Pinmei followed her gaze and caught sight of the gold silk robe. At Yishan's feet was the body of the emperor.

The form was unmoving. The emperor's face was frozen in a glare, and his arms were locked in an empty grip, as if even in his final moments he was grasping. Pinmei, again, felt a strange pang of pity.

"I know," Amah said, touching Pinmei's shoulder. "So much life but so little happiness. Perhaps the peace he never sought in life will find him in death."

"Is...is he dead?" Pinmei asked.

"Dead enough," Yishan said, and motioned her and Amah away. When they were far enough, the old man tossed the white-rabbit rice bowl at the emperor's lifeless body. As the bowl spun in the air, it grew and grew. When it finally fell upon the ground, it covered the emperor completely and turned into a mountain!

They stood at the foot of it and, for a moment, all Pinmei could do was gaze upward.

The old man grunted. "Not much of a mountain, is it?" he said in a familiar mocking tone. "More a hill, really."

Pinmei stared at him in bewilderment.

"But I thought..." she said. "The Paper said the emperor would be immortal."

"And so he will be," the old man said. "But not the way he thought."

"How?" Pinmei asked.

"Why don't you ask the Paper?" Yishan said, his eyes twinkling.

Pinmei took the Paper from her sleeve and unfolded it. A single line of words formed on the page. It was the same word, over and over again and to Pinmei's surprise, she could read it. The word was *Stories*.

"B-but..." Pinmei stuttered. "How will stories make the emperor immortal?"

Yishan laughed his bold and irreverent laugh. "How do you think?" he said. "The emperor was always trying to steal immortality. He never understood immortality is a gift that has to be given. A gift you will give him, even though he does not deserve it."

"Me?" Pinmei said. "I will give him immortality?"

"Yes, you, my friend I will never forget," Yishan said, and his wrinkled hands grasped hers. "And that is truly the only immortality that matters."

He released her, and as he bowed his head at Amah, Pinmei saw that instead of the red string, the jade bracelet was on her wrist. As she lifted her arm to look at it in the moonlight, she saw the old man was walking up the mountain. Yishan was leaving.

"Yishan!" Pinmei cried. "Will we see you again?"

He turned and grinned at her. "Every night," he said, cocking his head at the huge moon above. As Pinmei looked up at it, she thought she saw the silhouette of a rabbit sitting at the top of the mountain, waiting. Yishan's smile turned soft. He swung the Iron Rod to point up at the sky beyond them. "Look," he said.

They turned. A silver mist was rising from the snow and a delicate arc of light had formed above them. Tints of rose and gold and violet were washed upon it as if painted by the softest brush. It glowed with the light of the Sea King's palace, shimmered with the reflected colors of

Lady Meng's tear, and shone with the gentle splendor of the moon itself. Pinmei knew, of all the wonders she had seen on her journey, this rainbow by the light of the moon was the loveliest of them all.

Amah looked at her, eyes glistening. "Nuwa is smiling at us," she whispered. Pinmei nodded and, almost in unison, they turned back to see Yishan.

But he was gone. A warm breeze blew around them, and water was dripping like strings of pearls from melting icicles. The swallows, drowsy from their long naps as mussels, were singing, and a silver sea of clouds had drifted up to where the mountain met the moon.

Amah turned to Pinmei. "Let's leave this place," she said. "Do you know the way?"

Pinmei took her grandmother's arm.

"Yes," Pinmei said, and she smiled. "I'll take you."

CHAPTER
75

He was free.

He leaped on the wind, drinking in the delicious cold air. It flew him upward, higher and higher, until he burst through the thick clouds to where the sky flowed into the edge of the sea.

Ah, the black waters! He let it wash over him. Wonderful, wonderful water! The cool, tranquil blackness.

A thin wave coiled toward him. It was the snake. It looked at the tortoise with shining eyes, and he let it wrap around him in a loving embrace.

Below, the moon floated and the stars swam.

The Black Tortoise of Winter had returned home.

CHAPTER

76

In the City of Bright Moonlight, after the snow had melted away, a boy—or was he a man?—leaned heavily on a stick and shuffled down the Long Walkway to a pavilion. Panting, he rested on its railing. Above, the sky was the brilliant blue court artists could only imagine, and the sun was so warm he was glad to have the shade. He smiled to himself. What a feeling, to be too warm!

"Sifen!" a voice called his name. "Sifen!"

The boy turned and his smile widened. It was Yanna.

"We heard from Old Sai and Suya," Yanna called out

as she ran to him. "They said some men have already returned to the village."

"Good," Sifen said. Yanna sat down next to him.

"I bet all the men will be back soon," Yanna said. "Now that the Vast Wall is abandoned, men have been streaming into the city every day!"

"Has the palace provided for them?" Sifen asked.

"We don't have to," Yanna said. "What used to be the House of Wu has opened its doors to all travelers—the new owner, I guess she used to be the servant there—is truly a hero to..."

Yanna stopped in midsentence and rose, looking down the corridor. Sifen pushed himself up with his stick to follow her gaze. Three figures were walking toward them. The bright sun cast them in shadow, but he could see the shapes of a girl, an aged man, and an old woman.

"Who is it?" he asked Yanna.

"My...my...my father!" Yanna almost shrieked, the words trailing behind her as she burst forward, running faster than a flying dragon, to meet the visitors. The silhouette of the man also broke away from his companions, rushing toward Yanna with open arms. The two embraced tightly, laughing and crying at the same time, and Sifen could not help doing the same at the pure joy of their reunion. Even the peonies seemed to be exploding with happiness, their vibrant colors radiating in the sun.

The elderly woman and the young girl stepped forward, their faces also smiling with delight. The boy cocked his head. Did the girl seem familiar? Now she was walking toward him, calling his name. Yes! Now he knew her! She was...

"The Storyteller's granddaughter!" Sifen laughed. "What are you doing here?"

"Sifen!" Pinmei cried out. "I was about to ask you the same question!"

"Well, I asked first," Sifen said, grasping Pinmei's arm.

"We are here to return the stonecutter to his daughter," Amah said, "and to return a special paper to the king of the City of Bright Moonlight."

"My father is at his Pavilion of Solitude," Sifen said, waving his hand toward a remote building far down the lakeside, "painting as usual."

"Your father?" Pinmei said, and shook her head as she looked at Sifen's gleeful face. "The king of the City of Bright Moonlight is your father? I should have known."

Sifen continued to grin, but then, as if remembering his manners, he bowed to Amah. "You must be the Storyteller," he said, and then looked at Pinmei with sudden concern. "Where is your friend? The boy in red?"

"He too had to return something," Pinmei said. "But he is probably home now."

"As I am home now too," Sifen said, and if it was at all possible, his grin grew broader, as if trying to include the entire garden and sky. "But tell me: What happened? You made it to the city, obviously. Did anything happen on your travels? And what is it your friend had to return?"

"Ahh, young man," Amah said. "That is quite a story."

"Good!" Sifen said, and he looked at Pinmei. "You know I love stories."

Amah smiled and sat down.

Pinmei, however, looked at the decorated beam above her. It was a painting of an old man on a mountain, looking at the sea below. A sea dragon roared up from the waves with a maiden of extraordinary beauty by its side, her arm extended as if she had just caught something. All the creatures of the sea, from a graceful *longma* to a smiling fish, were bowing toward the mountain in gratitude. Above the sun—or was it the moon?—a rainbow arched in the sky. The painting was so detailed Pinmei could even see that between the fingers of the maiden's outstretched hand was a thin silver needle.

"Come, then!" Sifen said as Yanna and the stonecutter joined. "Tell the story!"

Pinmei looked down from the painting and saw the eyes of Yanna and the stonecutter, Sifen, and even Amah watching her eagerly. Amah patted her leg.

"Yes," Amah said, her smile broadening, "tell the story."

"I will," Pinmei said, and sat down.

Outside the pavilion, the glowing flowers repeated the colors of the painted rainbow, and the white clouds above echoed the cresting waves of water. Two butterflies, red and blue, flitted together as if writing poems in the air. *I will never forget*, Yishan had said, *and that is truly the only immortality that matters.*

Finally understanding, Pinmei closed her eyes, the memories of all she had lost and gained weaving around her in a glorious, invisible tapestry. When she opened her eyes, the others were still staring at her, waiting for her to start the story.

Pinmei smiled and began. "When the sea turned to silver..."

As a child, one of the few things I learned in Chinese was how to count to ten. However, even though I could rattle off the numbers, I did not see the magic in them. It was only as an adult that I learned that even humble numbers have a rich history in Chinese culture. Many of them are homophones, suggesting other words when spoken aloud, and the most popular of them are the numbers six, eight, and nine. The number six (*liù*) sounds like the word for "smooth" or "peaceful"; eight (*bā*) recalls the word for "fortune" and nine (*jiǔ*) sounds like the word for "forever." These are the auspicious numbers—hidden in Chinese paintings, used in emperors' robes, and picked for special dates and license plates. I have an especially vivid memory of my dinner companions in Hong Kong broadly grinning when the bill arrived with numerous sixes and nines. "We are so lucky!" one announced proudly.

After my first husband, Robert, died of cancer, I thought a great deal about life and what I wished from it. Strangely, it was these numbers that began to guide me. For, what were these numbers but symbols of what we want and wish for each other? Peace (six), good fortune (eight), and longevity (nine) are what the ancient Chinese decided make a truly lucky life.

But how does one get these...these elusive desires? With a

hubris given to authors, I decided upon my personal answers and put them in my books. In *Where the Mountain Meets the Moon*, Minli discovers the secret to good fortune—representing the number eight. Rendi finds the secret to peace in *Starry River of the Sky*, symbolized by the number six. And this book signifies the number nine, allowing Pinmei to learn that stories are the secret to immortality.

Why stories? Recently, a dear friend of mine's husband also died. At his memorial, all found solace in sharing stories about him. Many were stories I had never heard before, and I found myself wondering how many more there were that I didn't know. How many of Robert's stories had I not known? How many were now gone?

Because stories are how we share our lives and what we truly mourn when they are lost. Stories are what connect us to our past and carry us to our future. They are what we cherish and what we remember. They are why I write my books and why I offer them as my humble gift to you.

I hope you find them as much of a treasure as I did.

Some of the books that inspired
WHEN THE SEA
TURNED TO SILVER

Casanova, Mary. *The Hunter: A Chinese Folktale.* New York: Atheneum Books for Young Readers, 2000.

Cheney, Cora. *Tales from a Taiwan Kitchen.* New York: Dodd, Mead, 1976.

Courlander, Harold. *The Tiger's Whisker and Other Tales and Legends from Asia and the Pacific.* New York: Harcourt, Brace & World, Inc., 1959.

Daming, Zhang. *The Stories Behind the Long Corridor Paintings at the Summer Palace.* Beijing: New World Press, 2002.

Demi. *The Empty Pot.* New York: Henry Holt and Company, 1990.

Demi. *Under the Shade of the Mulberry Tree.* New York: Prentice Hall, 1979.

Handa, Lin and Cao Yuzhang. *Tales from 5000 Years of Chinese History Volume I.* New York: Better Link Press, 2010.

Jagendorf, M. A. and Virginia Weng. *The Magic Boat and Other Chinese Folk Stories*. New York: Vanguard Press, 1980.

Krasno, Rena, and Yeng-Fong Chiang. *Cloud Weavers: Ancient Chinese Legends*. Berkeley, CA: Pacific View Press, 2003.

Liyi, He. *The Spring of Butterflies and Other Chinese Folk Tales*. New York: Lothrop, Lee & Shepard Books, 1986.

Lobb, Fred H. *The Wonderful Treasure Horse: Mongolian, Manchu and Turkic Folktales from China*. Xlibris Corporation, 2000.

Man Ho, Kwok and Joanne O'Brien, eds. and trans. *The Eight Immortals of Taoism: Legends and Fables of Popular Taoism*. New York: Meridian, 1990.

Manton, Jo, and Robert Gittings. *The Flying Horses: Tales from China*. New York: Henry Holt and Company, 1977.

Sanders, Tao Tao Liu. *Dragons, Gods & Spirits from Chinese Mythology*. New York: Schocken Books, 1980.

Wang, Rosalind C. *The Fourth Question: A Chinese Tale*. New York: Holiday House, 1991.

Wong, Eva. *Tales of the Dancing Dragon: Stories of the Tao*. Boston: Shambhala Publications, Inc., 2007.

Wong, Eva. *Tales of the Taoist Immortals*. Boston: Shambhala Publications, Inc., 2001.

Yacowitz, Caryn. *The Jade Stone: a Chinese Folktale*. New York: Holiday House, 1992.